W9-CQG-042

"It's a good thing I can't get up out of this bed."

Joan sensed something ominous beneath Griff's even tone. "Oh?"

"Because I'm tempted to shake you silly. But then," he added wryly, "I'd probably just wind up kissing you."

Her mouth fell open, and he had the audacity to grin.

"You see, I have a temper, too, but I have sense enough to know I'd be better served by the kissing, and so, I think, would you."

"Of all the conceited, arrogant things to say!"

He shook his head, the glint of devilment in his blue eyes. "Won't wash, Jo. You're a woman who's been without a man far too long, and we both know that if you weren't attracted to me, you wouldn't be wringing your hands right now."

Dear Reader,

Happy Valentine's Day! We couldn't send you flowers or chocolate hearts, but here are six wonderful new stories that capture all the magic of falling in love.

Clay Rutledge is the *Father in the Middle* in this emotional story from Phyllis Halldorson. This FABULOUS FATHER needed a new nanny for his little girl. But when he hired pretty Tamara Houston, he didn't know his adopted daughter was the child she'd once given up.

Arlene James continues her heartwarming series, THIS SIDE OF HEAVEN, with *The Rogue Who Came to Stay.* When rodeo champ Griff Shaw came home to find Joan Burton and her daughter living in his house, he couldn't turn them out. But did Joan dare share a roof with this rugged rogue?

There's mischief and romance when two sisters trade places and find love in Carolyn Zane's duet SISTER SWITCH. Meet the first half of this dazzling duo this month in *Unwilling Wife.*

In Patricia Thayer's latest book, Lafe Colter has his heart set on Michelle Royer—the one woman who wants nothing to do with him! Will *The Cowboy's Courtship* end in marriage?

Rounding out the month, Geeta Kingsley brings us *Daddy's Little Girl* and Megan McAllister finds a *Family in the Making* when she moves next door to handsome Sam Armstrong and his adorable kids in a new book by Dani Criss.

Look for more great books in the coming months from favorite authors like Diana Palmer, Elizabeth August, Suzanne Carey and many more.

Happy Reading!

Anne Canadeo
Senior Editor
Silhouette Books

Please address questions and book requests to:
Silhouette Reader Service
U.S.: 3010 Walden Ave., P.O. Box 1325, Buffalo, NY 14269
Canadian: P.O. Box 609, Fort Erie, Ont. L2A 5X3

THE ROGUE WHO CAME TO STAY

Arlene James

Silhouette ROMANCE™
Published by Silhouette Books
America's Publisher of Contemporary Romance

If you purchased this book without a cover you should be aware that this book is stolen property. It was reported as "unsold and destroyed" to the publisher, and neither the author nor the publisher has received any payment for this "stripped book."

SILHOUETTE BOOKS

ISBN 0-373-19061-1

THE ROGUE WHO CAME TO STAY

Copyright © 1995 by Arlene James

All rights reserved. Except for use in any review, the reproduction or utilization of this work in whole or in part in any form by any electronic, mechanical or other means, now known or hereafter invented, including xerography, photocopying and recording, or in any information storage or retrieval system, is forbidden without the written permission of the editorial office, Silhouette Books, 300 East 42nd Street, New York, NY 10017 U.S.A.

All characters in this book have no existence outside the imagination of the author and have no relation whatsoever to anyone bearing the same name or names. They are not even distantly inspired by any individual known or unknown to the author, and all incidents are pure invention.

This edition published by arrangement with Harlequin Enterprises B.V.

® and TM are trademarks of Harlequin Enterprises B. V., used under license. Trademarks indicated with ® are registered in the United States Patent and Trademark Office, the Canadian Trade Marks Office and in other countries.

Printed in U.S.A.

Books by Arlene James

Silhouette Romance

City Girl #141
No Easy Conquest #235
Two of a Kind #253
A Meeting of Hearts #327
An Obvious Virtue #384
Now or Never #404
Reason Enough #421
The Right Moves #446
Strange Bedfellows #471
The Private Garden #495
The Boy Next Door #518
Under a Desert Sky #559
A Delicate Balance #578
The Discerning Heart #614
Dream of a Lifetime #661
Finally Home #687
A Perfect Gentleman #705
Family Man #728
A Man of His Word #770
Tough Guy #806
Gold Digger #830
Palace City Prince #866
**The Perfect Wedding* #962
**An Old-Fashioned Love* #968
**A Wife Worth Waiting For* #974
Mail-order Brood #1024
**The Rogue Who Came To Stay* #1061

*This Side of Heaven

Silhouette Special Edition

A Rumor of Love #664
Husband in the Making #776
With Baby in Mind #869

ARLENE JAMES

grew up in Oklahoma and has lived all over the South. In 1976 she married "the most romantic man in the world." The author enjoys traveling with her husband, but writing has always been her chief pastime.

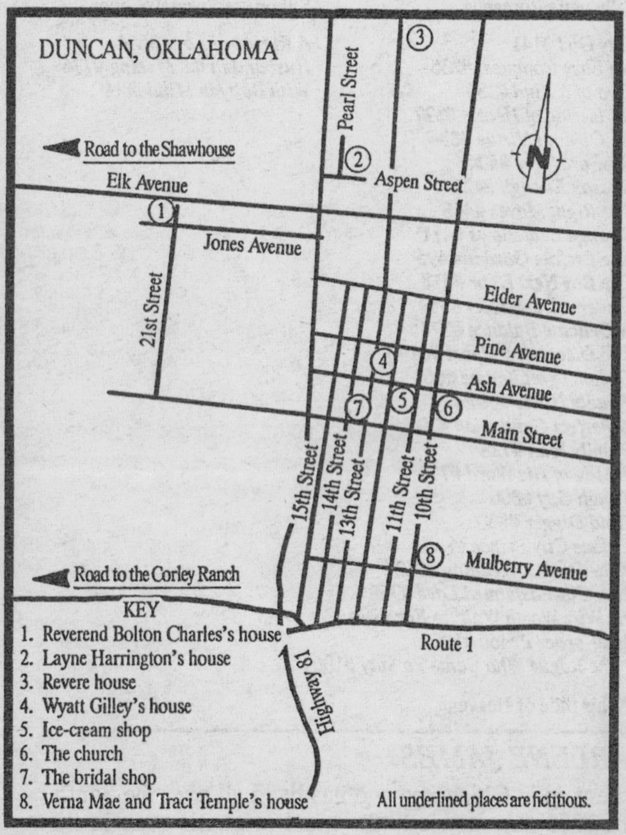
DUNCAN, OKLAHOMA
Road to the Shawhouse
Elk Avenue
Pearl Street
Aspen Street
Jones Avenue
21st Street
Elder Avenue
Pine Avenue
Ash Avenue
Main Street
15th Street
14th Street
13th Street
11th Street
10th Street
Mulberry Avenue
Road to the Corley Ranch
Route 1
Highway 81
KEY
1. Reverend Bolton Charles's house
2. Layne Harrington's house
3. Revere house
4. Wyatt Gilley's house
5. Ice-cream shop
6. The church
7. The bridal shop
8. Verna Mae and Traci Temple's house
All underlined places are fictitious.

Chapter One

"Me-e-r-r-ry Christmas to-o-o you-u-u!"

Joan sighed and fought the impulse to open her eyes, dimly aware that someone somewhere...someone near enough to disturb her sleep was shouting....

"Merry Chr-r-r-istmas to yo-o-ou!"

No, singing...very badly off-key.

"Merry Chri-i-istmas, dear Grandma Frankie-e-e!"

Frankie?

"Merry Christmas to—"

She sat up abruptly. Frankie. *Grandma* Frankie.

"You— Ow! Watch it! Damn!"

Joan pushed her wild red hair out of her face, her mind suddenly racing. Only one person in the world could call Frankie Thom "Grandma." The wretch. Here? Now?

Even as she heard the bell chiming and the blows upon the front door, she couldn't seem to grasp the notion that Griff Shaw might have come home. He wouldn't. Frankie had said so. The national rodeo finals were held just before

Christmas every year, and Griff Shaw always wanted, needed, to vacation right afterward. He never came home. Frankie had said quite clearly that her grandson's idea of a vacation paradise was a glamorous place with nonstop nightlife and nonstop women. Duncan, Oklahoma, was just too tame for a world champion bull rider. Frankie had said so.

A crash from below put a sudden end to Joan's rationalizations. She leapt from the bed, mechanically threw back her unruly mop of hair, grabbed her heavy terry-cloth robe from the small bedside chair and slung it on over her nightgown. She raced barefoot for the stairs, pausing on the landing only long enough to pull her daughter's door closed before flying down the steps, her robe billowing behind her. Thankfully Danna was a heavy sleeper, but the curse words and laughter booming up through the stairwell were loud enough to wake the neighbors, let alone her delicate little daughter. At the bottom of the stairs, her gaze turned into the living room, and she froze. There were three cowboys in her house, and one of them was rolling around on the floor in an apparent drunken stupor, while the other two slapped their thighs and laughed at him.

"Come on, man, get up!" one of them urged.

"He couldn't get up if his life depended on it," the other scoffed. "Besides being drunk as a skunk, he's all ripped up."

"Hell," sighed the first, pushing his hat back. "I forgot. Damn bull."

Just as Joan was considering whether or not she could make it past them to the phone in order to call the police, one of them glanced over his shoulder. His brows went up into the crown of his hat, and he elbowed the other, who whipped around so wildly that he almost wound up on the floor next to his buddy.

"Ma'am," the first said, politely doffing his hat.

Joan licked her lips. "Wh-who are you?"

The cowboy grinned. "Me? Why, I'm Casey Ashford," he said with delight, "and this here's Benny Butler, *the* Benny Butler, and that's Griff."

The names, with the exception of the last, meant nothing to her, but it was obvious from the accompanying grins that they were expected to. No doubt these two were part of the rodeo cowboy elite, but unlike most of the local population, Joan didn't keep up with the sport. And she couldn't be too impressed, considering what she knew about the great bull rider, Griff Shaw. Not that Frankie wasn't proud of him. She spoke often about her famous grandson, about how generous he was with his winnings, about his talent and success, his doggedness and wit, about how he'd known his own mind from a very young age and how nothing could turn him from his determined course. But Frankie was pretty much an open book, and she spoke, too, about how seldom she saw the boy she'd raised to manhood, about his wild ways and dangerous antics and about her despair of ever seeing him safe and settled before she departed this world. Now there he was, rolling around on the living room rug. The rat had finally come home to visit, and his grandmother wasn't even here.

She turned her attention back to the two standing cowboys, saw the speculative glances they traded, then quickly wrapped her robe tightly around her and knotted the sash. "Now then, explain yourselves," she said sternly, "or would you rather I just went ahead and called the police?"

They looked shocked. "What'd you want to do that for?" one demanded.

"Hey," the other said, "you better get Grandma Frankie down here right now."

Joan folded her arms, very aware that for all intents and purposes she was alone here with these men, but they didn't know that and she meant to keep it that way. "Frankie Thom is in Florida," she said very precisely, careful not to display the least discomfort. "The house has been leased. Now I want you out of here before you wake everyone in the neighborhood." She stepped aside, but no one moved toward the door.

"Hellfire," the one called Casey said, his hand going to the back of his neck.

The other joined in, adding, "Oh, man! What do we do now?"

"Can't take him with us," Casey said reasonably.

"Not in the shape he's in," the other—Barry?—concurred.

Casey Whoever pointed to the floor, where the drunken cowboy had stilled and was now breathing easily and deeply as if preparing to snore. "Boy needs nursing," he insisted.

Joan did a more thorough perusal. The downed cowboy was wearing a navy blue sling against a black shirt, his bandaged right arm cradled within it. His hat had been knocked off and lay at an angle across his face and he was sprawled awkwardly atop one of a pair of crutches, but there was no sign of a cast beneath his snug jeans. He did not, in fact, seem in any real distress.

Unmoved, she lifted her gaze back to Casey. "If he's in such bad shape, maybe you ought to take him to the hospital."

"Won't keep him in the hospital," Barry said. Or was it Benny? Yes, it was Benny.

"And why not?" she asked.

"No insurance," Casey explained, a woeful expression on his face.

"It's a damned scandal," Benny added solemnly.

"No insurance company in the nation will cover a rodeo cowboy," Casey vowed.

"Not if he makes a living climbing on wild bulls three or four times a week," Benny said with obvious relish.

Casey grinned. "Just 'cause he breaks a few bones every year."

Benny chuckled. "Got to have a few stitches now and again."

"Some nasty bruises to impress the girls with," Casey said, jabbing an elbow at his buddy.

"A gash or two that needs kissing! The man could sure use some expert nursing," Benny howled.

Joan rolled her eyes as they threw their arms around one another, guffawing. Benny sent Joan a wink from beneath the brim of his hat.

The *man,* apparently, was Griff Shaw. He didn't need a nurse; he needed an angel, one who could scrub up his blighted soul. "All right, all right!" she interrupted sternly. "So he's a little beaten up. I'm sure some silly female somewhere will be delighted to take him in. Meanwhile, I'm losing sleep and my . . . family . . . will be doing the same unless you take this *party* elsewhere."

"But there is nowhere else," Casey insisted, his smile fading.

She lifted a brow. "That's not my problem. Now I want you out of here. Go, or I'll call the police. I mean it."

"Okay, okay!" Benny soothed, straightening and wiping his hands down his shirtfront. "Don't get your tail in a knot!"

"Grandma always put us up for the night," Casey grumbled.

"Grandma is not here!" Joan snapped. "And I don't have room for three rude cowboys, but I'm sure they could find space in the county jail!"

"We're going!" Casey shouted, then abruptly lowered his voice. "Cab's waiting, anyhow." He shook his head. "Hot red! Never saw one that didn't have a temper. Come on, Ben. Let's get outta here. I'm fancying a brunette myself."

"You always fancy brunettes," Benny complained. "What's wrong with an occasional blonde?"

"We'll get two," Casey assured him, pulling him forward. "Brown for me, blond for you. And no redheads!" he added resentfully as they passed by Joan.

The smell of whiskey nearly knocked her over. She reeled backward, turning as they clopped their heavy boots over the polished parquet of the entry.

"S'pose she'll take care of him?" Benny asked worriedly.

Casey snorted. "Don't reckon we've got a choice either way. There's nowhere else for him to go."

The *him* suddenly flailed, muttering nonsense. It struck Joan then that they were actually leaving Griff Shaw behind! She whirled and gaped at him. He moaned, rocking side to side, gritted his teeth then seemed to settle down again.

"Wait!" she cried, whirling back to the other two men. They stopped at the door and turned to face her.

"Go! Wait! Make up your mind!" Benny said, exasperated.

She ignored him, making her appeal to Casey, who seemed the dominant bozo. "You can't leave him here! You have to take him with you!"

Casey pushed his hat forward. "Lady, we brought him home so he could get the care he needs. He can't go back out on the road now, and we can't stay with him."

Benny nodded. "We've got to be in Oklahoma City in the morning to catch the plane to Vegas."

"There's one more round in the finals," Casey explained with the same patience he'd show a dull-witted child, "and with Griff out of the way, me and Benny got equal chances of coming out on top."

"He'd want us to ride," Benny insisted. "He'd do the same in our place." He scratched his chin. "On the other hand, he's liable to be mad as a hornet when he sobers up. See, we had to get him drunk to get him on the plane."

She opened her mouth to tell them that she just couldn't worry about it. Griff Shaw was not her responsibility. But Casey shook his head stubbornly. "We can't take him back. He qualified before he wrecked. It was maybe his best ride ever."

"Helluva ride," Benny agreed.

"Why, it'd take me and Ben and every other cowboy in Nevada to keep him from riding in the final go-round," Casey said. "Old Griff's not too reasonable about something like this. He don't like to be beat, not by no bull he's already counted eight on."

Benny screwed up his face. "Oh, it was a nasty business, though. That bull, he got personal, wrecked Griff real bad."

Joan lifted her hands in supplication. "You don't understand—"

Casey snatched the hat from his head and poked at her with it. "You don't understand, Red! Griff don't know when to quit. He nearly got killed, but he'd sure as breathing get right back on again, and the doctors in Vegas said he didn't dare until he heals up."

"We didn't bring him home just for healing," Benny said flatly. "We brought him home to keep him from getting killed."

Joan digested that in silence. This *was* Griff Shaw's house. She supposed that it was, technically, his home. But when she'd moved into the house, Frankie had assured her... Frankie had *promised*... She sighed. It didn't really matter what Frankie had said. She couldn't turn an injured man out of his own house, not that she intended to play Florence Nightingale for him. Nothing of the sort. But if he really had nowhere else to go... Loathing her capitulation, she fixed the two cowboy-hatted miscreants with a scathing glare. "All right," she muttered grimly. "He can stay the night. Tomorrow I'll—"

"Hallelujah!" Casey exclaimed, yanking open the front door and cramming his hat down on his head. Cold air nipped at her toes. She snatched them back under the hem of her robe.

"Thank you, ma'am," Benny said, fast on Casey's heels. Then suddenly he stopped and reversed course. "Almost forgot." He patted down his pockets, lifted the flap of one on his shirt and fished something out. "Griff's key," he said, stepping forward and pressing it into her hand. Awkwardly he doffed his hat and beat a hasty retreat. A moment later, the door closed behind him. Joan frowned and looked down at the key in her hand.

His key. But of course he'd have a key. It was his house after all. His house, but *her* home, hers and Danna's, at least until Frankie got back from Florida in the spring. He groaned, and Joan joined him, putting her head back against the wall. What a mess! She should have known this would happen. There was something about her that drew scoundrels and jerks like vultures to carrion. Well, not this time. He could stay the night where he was, but tomorrow... Tomorrow she'd think of something else.

Then she thought of her daughter. Danna shouldn't have to witness the sorry scene he was bound to make in the morning. If the whiskey fumes emanating from the floor were any indication, he was going to have one jim-dandy of a hangover, and if his friends were right, he was going to be mad to boot. Well, he wouldn't be the only one. She was mad enough already to kick him, and he hadn't even opened his mouth yet. Still and all, she wouldn't kick a man when he was down. In fact, she couldn't just leave him there on the floor like that, especially if he was hurt.

She slipped his key into her robe pocket and turned back into the living room. The sight of him lying there was blatantly incongruous with the orderly room and gaily decorated tree in the window. She studied his lean frame. He didn't look hurt except for that sling, but he was drunk enough to be deathly sick at the very least. He was on his back, having worked himself off the crutch, his legs stretched out and his free arm flung over his face, his hat beside his head. Maybe she should just leave him after all. He obviously wouldn't know the difference. But her heart was softer than it should be, and she was too tired to fight it.

She went into the downstairs bedroom that opened up beneath the stairwell. This was Frankie's room, and many of her things still remained there. It had the one full bath in the house and the largest closet, but Joan hadn't seen any reason to move into it herself. She much preferred to be upstairs close to her daughter, and she could always come down and soak in the tub when she wanted to. Actually, a long, hot soak sounded pretty good. Her feet were cold and her nerves were jangled, but it was the middle of the night, and she'd undoubtedly need a clear mind in the morning. She'd have to find some solution to this dilemma, but she wasn't going to think about it now.

She pulled a blanket and pillow from Frankie's bed and carried them to the living room. Griff Shaw lay exactly as she'd left him, dead to the world. He looked impossibly tall stretched out on the carpet, tall and lean and muscled, very like Daniel. Daniel. Disgusted at the mere thought of her ex-husband, she threw the blanket over the cowboy, then knelt to lift his head and slide the pillow beneath it. His arm fell away, and he moaned, but made no protest. She couldn't help noticing that he was a handsome man. Weren't they all, the stinkers, the bounders, the cads? From the looks of him, this one was one of the worst. Like the rest of him, his face was lean and sculpted, the bone structure prominent, his mouth firm and full. There was a thin scar beneath his left eyebrow. She wouldn't have noticed it except that it was so pale against the bronzed flesh of his face and the chocolate-dark slash of his brow. She wondered if he'd gotten it riding or carousing. More likely the latter, she told herself, pushing up to her full height.

Suddenly his hand shot out and clamped around her ankle. His eyes opened to slits. "Hey, sugar, don' go 'way," he slurred. "Jus' give me minute. I'll be . . ." His words trailed off, and his eyes drifted closed again.

Joan shook her head and snatched her ankle from his grasp, which had loosened as he'd drifted back into his alcohol-induced slumber. *Tomorrow,* she told him silently, *you're out of here, buster.* She had no use for a man like him, and only minimal pity. She knew his kind well enough, too well, and she had no desire to know another. One was more than enough, thank you. In fact, one had been too much. And in light of that experience, she couldn't believe what she was doing now, but what choice did she have? He might be beneath contempt, but he was also injured, and at the moment that took precedence.

She walked to the doorway and flipped the wall switches, turning off table lamps as well as the twinkling lights on the Christmas tree, but then she thought better of leaving him in the dark alone. He was bound to wonder where he was when he awoke, and she didn't want to take a chance on his falling over something. She flipped the tree lights back on and stood for a moment in the soft, colored glow. She wondered where Daniel was tonight and what he was doing. Did he ever think of his daughter? Did he ever regret the choices he had made? Better not to know. Knowing would likely bring only pain, and she'd had her quota for a whole lifetime already. The Reverend Bolton Charles said it was wrong not to forgive, that she had to let it go and get on with her life, but he had never loved and trusted and had it all flung back in his face. He'd never tried to explain to a wide-eyed little girl why her daddy didn't call or come or even acknowledge her existence.

But that wasn't Daniel lying there. That was Frankie Thom's grandson, and he couldn't be all bad and still belong to Frankie. No, that great lady would have instilled *some* degree of goodness in him. She allowed herself to hope for a moment that it was so, that he didn't have a little girl somewhere hoping and praying for a word of acceptance, for a gesture of remembrance from her very own daddy. She allowed herself to believe, for the night, that her world hadn't just been turned upside down.

Dawn had lifted the black of night and left in its place a heavy gray light. Joan blinked and stretched, forgetting the troubled dreams that had maligned her sleep, and snuggled deeper into the soft warmth of her bed. Then a wild, grating cry rent the serenity, and her eyes flew open as she jerked upright in the bed. Griff Shaw. Downstairs. Pain. The thoughts flashed through her mind as she leapt from the bed and ran.

He cried out again. It was the most agonized sound she had ever heard, the most heartrending, the most frightening. She bounded down the stairs and across the entry, her hair and gown flying. The man had struggled up onto the coffee table with one elbow and was clawing at his belt buckle. He didn't even look at her, just demanded that she help him.

"Get 'em off! Get 'em off! God in heaven!" He put his head back and gritted his teeth, making harsh, guttural sounds deep in his throat. She knew instantly that he wanted his jeans off, that they were somehow contributing to his pain. There were tears on his face, and no one had to tell her that Griff Shaw, world-class bull rider, was the last man on the face of the earth to cry over any bearable agony.

Banishing modesty, she ripped his belt buckle free and went to work on his button fly. His good hand covered hers as he tried to help. She batted it away, got the last buttons free and shoved her hands beneath his arms, lifting with all her might. He cried out, but had the presence of mind to push upward with his good leg, catching his weight on his elbow. "Get 'em off!" he panted. "Peel 'em!" She grasped the edges of his waistband and yanked downward. He lifted his hips, demanding, "My leg! Get 'em off my leg!"

She yanked again and fell backward onto her bottom, pulling with all her might. He yelled and collapsed onto the table, scattering ribbon candy as the dish spun to the floor. Joan gaped at the nasty wound that wrapped around his hugely swollen right thigh as he struggled into a sitting position, cursing through clenched teeth. The bandage had been partially torn away, revealing the red, wet, puffy edges of ripped flesh held together by neat black stitches. No wonder he was in agony. The swelling was far too great for his pant leg to contain. He must have felt as if it were bursting!

He muttered something about his boots and pills and the torture used in hospitals. "I'll help you with your boots," she told him, getting to her knees, "but I don't know anything about any pills."

He put a hand to his head, keeping his elbows close to his body, and seemed to be trying to think. She grasped the boot on his good leg and pulled. He reared back in pain, but clamped his mouth shut on it and tugged his foot free. She dropped the boot to the floor. The other one was going to be a lot worse, and she knew it, but short of cutting it off, there was nothing else to do but pull on it. She sat back on her heels and considered.

"Can you lift it up and rest it on my knee?" He seemed not to have heard. She put her hand on his good arm and peered into his face. "If you can lift up your foot and rest it on my knee, I think I can work the boot off."

He nodded wearily, reached down with his left hand and laboriously lifted his right ankle. She guided it onto her knee and began the difficult process of coaxing the boot off. He groaned and gritted his teeth, his hand clasping her shoulder for support as she tugged and shifted, shifted and tugged. At last his heel slipped free, and she sat back to draw the boot off, hearing him catch his breath as she carefully lowered his leg. No sooner was his foot on the floor than he lifted it again and tried to lie back.

"Whoa, cowboy!" She shot up and grabbed him by the shirtfront. "You're not in bed, and you don't want to fall."

He looked around blearily. "Where'm I?"

"Never mind that now. I can't get you to the bedroom so you'll have to stay on the couch."

"All same t'me," he mumbled, waving his hand.

She could see only one way to do it. With luck he wouldn't even remember it later in the morning. She picked up the nearest crutch with one hand and took him by the wrist with the other. "Put your weight on your good leg and your arm around my shoulders."

He peered at her for a moment as if trying to put a name to her face, then wobbled a nod. He shifted his weight forward, put his foot on the floor and pushed. At the same time, she ducked under his arm and straightened, her own arm wrapped around his waist. He sucked in his breath, but his hand clamped around the top of her arm as he steadied himself. She positioned the crutch between them and gradually eased away.

"Can you stand there for a few seconds?"

"Sure, darlin'," he drawled, swaying precariously. "Damn, it hurts."

"I know, and I'm sorry. Just bear up a few seconds more."

He nodded, and she steadied him as best she could, then left him leaning on the crutch while she pushed the coffee table aside and kicked candy out of the way. He watched her, head bent. When she came back to slip her arm around his waist once more, he leaned close and said too loudly in her ear, "D'I know you?"

She turned her head away from his stale breath and answered brusquely, "No!"

He quirked one corner of his mouth up in a crooked grin. "Didn' think so. I 'member the good-lookin' ones."

She let the compliment roll off her without response. "You're not likely to remember anything ever again if you fall before I get you on that couch," she told him.

He took a deep breath and said, "Man, tha' ol' bull got me good, but I don' think I'm like to die for a li'l fall. 'Preciate it, though, if you'd keep a good hold on me."

From the glint in his eye, she supposed that was his idea of a pass, but she did not allow it to affect her. "We're going to back up a couple steps now," she said calmly. "You just lean on me and keep your weight on your good leg. Ready?"

"Yeah."

One hand on his waist, the other on the arm draped over her shoulders, she stepped back. He planted the crutch and hopped backward, his jaw clamped. They did it again. He was panting heavily as she turned him slightly and guided him down onto the couch. She took the crutch, and he sat there a moment in his shirttail and socks, gathering strength, his wounded leg stretched out before him, while she batted away throw pillows and propped up cushions. When she took hold of him again to ease him into a lying position, he was trembling violently from exhaustion and pain.

"Tell me about those pills again," she said, fixing one pillow beneath his knee and another beneath his ankle.

He lifted a hand to his head. "My kit," he said finally. "My gear, seems like Ben put 'em there."

She spread the blanket over him and pushed her hair back. "I'll have a look. You lie still."

He closed his eyes obediently, his face drawn and hard in the gentle light. She looked around the room, then walked out into the entry. Leaning in the corner behind the door was a black canvas duffel with a flap. She hauled it into the living room, surprised by its weight, and opened the top to lift out a wide, rough belt of some sort wrapped in leather strips fixed with metal rings. Next came a shirt and a pair of jeans folded together, some wadded socks wrapped in a pair of clean white briefs identical to the ones she had glimpsed beneath the long tail of the shirt he was wearing, and a shaving kit. The pills were in the kit—four separate bottles, two for pain, one for infection and the other for inflammation. She read the labels carefully, shook out the required doses and padded into the kitchen for a glass of water. He was holding his right shoulder and sucking air between his teeth when she came back.

"Here, take these." She held the pills in her palm. He looked up at her and opened his mouth. She tilted the first two in. He lifted his head, and she held the glass to his lips. He gulped and put his head back. "Again," she said.

It seemed to take the last strength he had. She watched him for a long moment, wondering if she should leave him even long enough to go upstairs for her robe. It was chilly on this gray December morning, and she was suddenly aware that she was standing there in nothing but a flimsy nightgown. He made no movement, no sound, but she could see that he was still in great pain. She decided she'd just give the pills a few minutes to work. She stood there, not knowing what to do and resenting the pity she was feeling. After what seemed a very long while, she turned quietly and walked toward the entry. She had just reached the doorway when he spoke.

"Hey, Red." His voice was husky and strained, but it seemed suddenly to skitter over her nerve endings with shocking intensity. She shook off the feeling as best she could and turned, saying nothing. He studied her through the narrow slits of his eyes, then closed them and said softly, "Thanks."

She stood there for a moment, her hands balled into fists, but she could not make herself say that he was welcome. She wished him no ill. Indeed, she felt a very real compassion because of his pain and weakness, but he was trouble. She knew it deep down in her bones, knew it as well as she knew her own name. And it wasn't fair. She'd had his kind of trouble once already, and she would not give way to it again. She would not allow him even a tiny piece of her heart, not even friendship. She couldn't. She just couldn't.

Resolutely she turned and walked away. When she came back again, hair brushed and held back with an elastic band, robe belted securely around her, slippers warming her feet, he was sleeping. His features had softened somewhat, despite the crease between his dark brows and the line that marred his forehead. He really was a fine-looking man, with his dark hair, pale blue eyes and finely sculpted features. He was well formed, lean and muscular. His hand lay against his shoulder, the palm wide, the fingers long and tapered and heavily knuckled—a strong hand. She took this all in dispassionately, as if from a great distance or through the long passage of time. What she saw only added to her determination to be rid of him as quickly as possible.

She went into the kitchen, made coffee and began planning what to do. She would have to call for a substitute to take her place at work. She couldn't leave him alone. In truth, from what she'd seen so far, he needed full-time nursing care, but surely she could arrange something until Frankie could get home from Florida. She hated to call Frankie. Not only would this news spoil her trip, but it could mean that she and Danna would once more be looking for some place to live. In fact, it seemed most likely. Perhaps the house would be big enough for all of them, but she and Danna simply could not stay in the same place with Griff Shaw indefinitely. It simply would not do. On the other hand, suitable rental property was rather dear around Duncan these days. She wouldn't find another affordable place half as nice as this one. If only she hadn't let the apartment go, but there was no sense in regretting what could not be changed. She'd just have to look for something else, but first she must notify Frankie and get some nursing help in here. As to the latter, she would call the Reverend Mr. Charles. Surely he could advise her. She liked and respected the young minister and his wife, Clarice, and it had been he who had introduced her to Frankie Thom in the first place.

Meanwhile, she'd call Danna's sitter and let her know that Danna wouldn't be coming over this morning. They might as well enjoy this rare weekday morning at home together. Thankfully tomorrow was Saturday, so she wouldn't have to worry about a substitute again for a couple of days. Surely by that time, Frankie would be home or she'd have arranged nursing care. So, at the worst, she was looking at three days of inconvenience. She could live with that.

She sipped her coffee, feeling immeasurably better, and got out her address book to hunt up the necessary numbers. She'd made too much of her earlier unease. After all, he couldn't really hurt her. No man would hurt her ever again.

Chapter Two

He wondered groggily which hurt worse, his head or his thigh, but then he took a deep breath and knew there was no contest really. He hurt like hell all over as he had for several days now, but the leg was incredibly painful. The pills took the edge off, wore the sensation down to a dull, glowing throb, but it always came back again with fresh fury. There was something else this morning, though, something unkindly familiar. His gut felt rubbery, and his throat burned. His mouth tasted like the bottom of a compost pile, and his head ached in new places. He lifted a hand to his temple and remembered the whiskey bottle that Benny had chucked into his lap after they'd left the hospital. He groaned. The last thing he needed now was a hangover, and he'd told those two that when they'd picked him up. But would they listen? No way. And it was a given that he didn't have sense enough to forgo the fun.

That had always been his problem. Fun sort of hunted him down, and he'd never had the strength to run the other way until the good time invariably transformed into a headache. And it was always his head that hurt.

Oh, but how they had howled for those next few hours! He seemed to remember a blonde in a convertible and another in a tight red sequined dress. She'd been standing on the corner, a long, filmy scarf in one hand, a tiny pocketbook in the other. He remembered telling Casey that even the prostitutes in Vegas were flashy. Had they hired her? He doubted it. That was not his style, but in all honesty he couldn't remember. He had been with a woman, he knew that, but a blonde didn't fit with the jumbled pictures in his head.

He sighed and carefully laid his good arm across his eyes. It was morning. He could feel the bright, brittle light behind his closed lids, but he was reluctant to admit it, knowing it would stab his bleary eyes unmercifully. He chose, instead, to assemble the flashes in his mind into a cohesive picture. She'd had red hair. He remembered that much. Bright red, wild, billowing long hair. And she'd worn something silky, something dark that had made the pale skin of her bare arms, legs and face seem to glow in the moonlight. Moonlight? No, colored light, soft colored light. A Christmas tree flashed across his mind's eye, a Christmas tree standing before a wide draped window like the one in Frank's house.

Grandma Frank's house.

He felt a sudden jolt of recognition, an eerie, growing awareness. Carefully he lifted his arm and opened his eyes to see... ceiling, white stuccoed ceiling like a million other ceilings he'd seen in his life. Bravely he turned his head and came face-to-face with...his redhead? He struggled up onto his elbow as far as his broken collarbone and ribs would allow and looked at her. She looked back, her expression changing not at all. He blinked and took careful inventory.

She was a child, a very young child, a fact which did not fit with the half-remembered images lurking within his brain. Still, she had that riotous red hair. It had been brushed back on top and secured with a pink barrette, but it fluffed out behind her head in soft, curly clouds. She had a Kewpie doll face, full cheeks and broad forehead, button nose, enormous brown eyes and a pink bow of a mouth above a small, pointy chin. Sitting cross-legged on the floor in a pink quilted robe and matching flannel nightgown with ruffles and bows, bunny heads on her feet, her tiny chin propped in one pudgy hand, she looked like a small princess from a fairy tale. He cleared his throat, found it desert dry and swallowed painfully. Without a word, she reached for a glass on a small table to one side and handed it to him.

Cute kid, he thought as he took the glass from her. Wondering whose child she was, he sipped the water, relieved that it didn't threaten to come right back up, and scanned the room. He was at Grandma's. He didn't know how it had happened, but here he was in Frankie's comfortable living room. He switched his gaze back to the girl and willed his voice to work.

"Hi."

She waggled her fingers at him, her calm stare never wavering. His arm was shaking with the effort of supporting his upper body weight. He needed to lie down again. She seemed to know it. Scooting forward, she took the glass from his hand and set it aside. He collapsed onto his pillow.

"What's your name, honey?"

"Danna."

"Dan?"

"Na."

He didn't get it. "What?"

"Danna. Dan-na."

"Oh. Well, hello, Danna. I'm Griff."

She shook her head. "Mr. Shaw," she said pointedly.

He chuckled at the formality, pain lancing through his head. "Okay, whatever. Now listen, go get Grandma Frankie for me, would you? I've got a he—er, heck of a headache."

She shook her head once again, more pronouncedly this time, the hair swishing about her shoulders.

He frowned. "Why not?"

She straightened. "Not here." And plopped her chin into her hand again.

Not here. Ah. He closed his eyes and breathed through the throbbing. He desperately wanted to bathe and brush his teeth and shave. Then he'd be wanting those pills again. Damn, but he hated having to take those things. He could remember a couple of times in the past hours—days?—when he'd have sold his soul to get them, though. He turned back to the girl. "Is there anyone who can help me up?"

She shook her head.

"No one?"

Abruptly she got up and sped away. He groaned, his head pounding, his thigh burning, ribs aching, wrist and collarbone twinging. Well, he'd just have to get himself up. He had no doubt that he could do so. Hadn't he always? He pulled as deep a breath as his ribs would allow and urged his body upward. Pain lanced through him and his head swam, but once sitting upright, he actually felt a little better. The sofa cushions were too soft to support his cracked ribs properly, but no doubt he'd be moved into more appropriate quarters before long. He hated to displace Frank, but her room was the most logical place for him. He didn't want to think about having to get up and down the stairs. He wondered idly why the munchkin was here, and where Frank was at this moment, not to mention Casey and Ben. Well, the most pressing matter at the moment was to find someone who could help take care of his immediate needs.

He looked around and spotted his crutches and jeans. Someone had folded his jeans neatly and wound his belt and laid it atop them, his championship belt buckle turned upward. Championship belt buckle. The championship! He groaned and swore. The finals! He'd missed the last go-round. Damn that bull! And blast Ben and Casey! He'd told them he wasn't leaving. He'd qualified, dammit. He could have finished in the money. All he'd have to have done was show up and sit the next bull long enough to clear the chute! He'd sworn he'd never miss a big-money ride due to injury. It was only eight seconds! Eight lousy seconds. He could hold his guts in with his hands for eight lousy seconds! Never mind that he couldn't have mounted without help, that he'd have had to endure unthinkable pain, that— Aw, hell, who was he kidding? He couldn't ride a rocking horse right now. He could hardly get himself to his feet, let alone properly dressed. Worse yet, that ravishing redhead had apparently been a figment of his imagination, unless...

He looked at his jeans again. A memory teased his mind. He saw a woman with a mature version of Danna's hair and face bending over him as she worked his buttons free. She'd been wearing...purple silk or something very like it, *not* pink flannel, and she'd had full breasts and good legs. He remembered that quite clearly now, and he seemed to remember something else, too. A foot. An ankle. His hand around her ankle?

He snatched up the closest crutch and angled it under his good arm. Holding his breath, he hurled himself upward and managed to plant the crutch well enough to take his weight as he swayed against it. He clenched his teeth and expelled his breath, waiting for the dizziness to pass and the pain to ease. After several moments, he switched the crutch to the other side. It would no doubt hurt like all get-out when he swung his weight onto it, but it was the only sensible way to manage. He took one tiny step and stopped. It wasn't as bad as he'd expected. He prepared himself for another, but just as he started forward, Danna reappeared.

Her eyes grew even larger when she saw him standing. He glanced down to be sure that he was decently covered by the tail of his shirt. Barely, but it would have to do. He managed another step forward, using his good leg and the crutch.

"Mommy said to wait," she announced importantly.

Mommy? He grinned, despite the all-enveloping pain. She wasn't a figment of his imagination, after all. He leaned on his good leg and peered down at her. She really was a doll. Her mother was bound to be a beauty. He didn't remember even an awareness of another man being around, but it was always better to be safe than sorry. He readjusted his weight and asked casually, "What about your daddy? What does he say?"

Danna cocked her head, brows drawing together. "He's not here."

"No? Well, where is he?"

She rubbed her hand over her face, smoothing back wisps of hair, and said, "Mexico."

His brows went up. "Mexico! What's he doing there?"

She linked her hands together and twisted them out in front of her. "I dunno. He lives with an old rich lady."

Several seconds ticked by while he absorbed that. When the conclusion came, it provoked a grin. "You mean...your mommy and daddy are divorced?"

She nodded. "He 'vorced Mommy and went away with that other lady. Papa said he was no better than a skunk."

Divorced. He couldn't keep the grin off his face. "Papa? That your grandfather?"

"Uh-huh."

"And where does he live?"

"Oklahoma City."

"Ah. Is that where you live, too?"

She laughed at him. "No, silly, I live here!"

"Here? In this house?" Could it get better than this?

She was nodding. "Yep. Want to see my room upstairs?"

He shook his head, smiling. "I don't think I'd better try that just yet. In fact, I think I'm going to be stuck downstairs for quite awhile. Tell you what, though, I'm going to brush my teeth, if it's all the same to you."

"You can't," she insisted. "Mommy said to wait."

"Oh, it'll be all right," he assured her, hobbling to his duffel. "I can manage that much, at least." He bent very carefully, his weight balanced on his good leg, and extracted his shaving kit, which thankfully lay right on top. Straightening, he paused to catch his breath. The little munchkin was staring at him, concern in her big brown eyes. Best to distract her. He put on his most ingratiating smile. "Say, little darlin', you don't have a newspaper around here do you?"

"It's outside. They throw it on the front yard."

"Oh, well, I sure would like to catch up on the local news. Don't suppose you'd run get it for me, would you? Can't go myself, you know."

She hitched her little shoulder in acquiescence, and his answering smile dazzled her so that she dazzled him back.

"That's my girl!" he said. "Oh, and be sure to put on a coat...and shoes and socks, maybe a hat of some sort...and mittens. You must have a pair of mittens." When she giggled, he winked at her. "I bet they've got bunnies on them, don't they?"

"No, kittens!"

"Kittens? Well, you put those kittens on, darlin', before you go out that door, okay?" She nodded and ran off to climb the stairs.

He didn't hesitate. He made his way through the entry and down the hall to Frank's bedroom door. Getting it open was a trick. He had to hold the heavy leather shaving kit in his teeth by the zipper slide, and that put pressure on his broken clavicle, but right then he'd have endured worse in order to brush the taste of last night's whiskey out of his mouth. He made quick work of it, transferred the kit to his hand once more and paused to catch his breath. He wondered if he could manage a shave. A shower sounded good, too, but that would have to wait until he could climb the stairs. Grandma Frankie's bath contained only a tub, while the bath upstairs contained only a shower. He didn't dare try that tub yet, either, but maybe he could sponge off. That ought to make him a little more attractive to the lady.

Mentally, he licked his chops at the prospect of getting to work on her. If that redhead proved as stirring as he seemed to remember and if she lived here with Frank as the little princess claimed, convalescence might well prove more enjoyable than he had imagined. He wondered, as he navigated the space between Frank's rosewood four-poster and the matching triple dresser, why Danna and her mommy were living with Grandma Frank and if it had anything to do with her father dumping her mother for a wealthy older woman. With that thought in his head, he clamped the zipper slide between his teeth, steeled himself, and wrenched open the bathroom door.

She was sitting in the white tub, a veritable vision of erotic beauty. Pink nipples crowned full, creamy breasts that rose proudly from an unbelievably narrow rib cage, and her bright, abundant hair was piled on top of her head in frothy clumps. One small hand had frozen in the process of sweeping damp tendrils off her slender neck, ivory skin gleaming wet. She did, indeed, possess a leaner, more refined version of her little daughter's face, but her mouth was lush and plum pink, and her eyes, now enormous with shock, were a lighter shade of brown, amber almost. His first thought was that Danna's father must be out of his mind. His second was that he somehow would have to find a way to get her into bed with Frankie none the wiser. He wasn't even aware that the shaving kit had bounced off the floor because his mouth was hanging open in awe, and he realized only belatedly—after the first shriek—that she had chucked the soap at him. It hit him in the chest and fell with a thunk at his feet. The shampoo bottle he actively tried to avoid by jerking back and to the side, and that proved his undoing, for it threw him off balance, and when he lunged forward again and attempted to plant the crutch in order to correct, the rubber butt clipped the bar of slippery soap.

He fell hard, twisting when he instinctively tried to catch his weight on his injured leg, and heard his own roar of pain vibrate through his head before everything went black. He opened his eyes only seconds later, burning all over with white-hot agony. She was kneeling at his side, an apricot-colored towel clasped to her chest.

"Don't move!" she yelled, and when she reached up to rip another towel from the bar overhead he caught a glimpse of sleek, pale flesh and the plump curve of bottom and thigh.

Even through the haze of pain he was male enough to regret that he was in no shape to take advantage of the situation. But then she lifted his leg to wrap the towel around it, and he stiffened and howled.

"You're bleeding!" she snapped at him.

He hurt too badly even to look for himself, but he clamped his jaw shut, determined not to embarrass himself more than he could help, and relaxed as well as he was able. She wrapped the towel around his thigh, amber eyes snapping.

"Of all the stupid, idiotic, ill-mannered, *unbelievable* things to do!"

He nodded in agreement with her, though he was uncertain which of them was the stupid, idiotic, ill-mannered, unbelievable one. True, he had barged in on her, but *she* had thrown the damned soap and shampoo bottle. None of that mattered at the moment, though. The bathroom floor was cold and hard, and he hurt like hell. All he wanted was a bed and a handful of wonder drugs. Gritting his teeth, he attempted to lift onto his elbow. "H-help me up."

"Be still, fool!" She put a hand in the middle of his chest and pushed.

He howled again and crumpled like a paper doll, gasping, "My ribs!"

Her mouth firmed grimly. She ran her hand down his torso none too gently, then grasped the edges of his shirt and ripped the snaps apart, revealing the pressure bandage about his rib cage.

It was laughable really, him there on the floor, stripped down to his skivvies and an open shirt, her bending over him clad in a towel, that glorious hair tumbling over one shoulder, and him incapacitated to the point where he couldn't even steal a kiss! God was punishing him. Frank had warned him, and she was right. It was torture, calculated torture. Let a bull stomp the stuffing out of him, then throw him in the way of a beautiful redhead with the obligatory temper. He couldn't stand it. He closed his eyes and moaned his misery.

"That's it!" she said crisply. "I'm calling an ambulance."

He wanted to laugh. He truly wanted to laugh. Instead he grabbed her wrist, grunting with the pain of the movement, and managed a no. She shook him off, insisting that he not compound his stupidity.

"You're bleeding," she repeated sternly, leaning down close to his face. "You've busted your stitches. You've probably broken another rib or cracked your skull or... worse. Now I'm calling an ambulance. *You* are going to stay still until it gets here, while *I* put on some clothes, and if you argue with me or try to get up from there or... or anything, I'll just finish the job you've started and toss the body out with the trash. Do you understand me?"

He actually managed a smile and a clever comeback. "Might be worth it," he grated out. "I doubt you could do murder and hang on to that towel at the same time."

She stood and smiled down at him, saying sweetly, "Want my towel, cowboy? Fine. You can have it, then." And she dropped it on his face. By the time he'd batted it off his head, she was gone. He actually chuckled, biting off the sound at the end as pain seared through him. He gasped air, holding his sides, and tried to relax. No point in fighting it, anyway. He wasn't going anywhere by himself. He could feel the sticky warmth of blood on his thigh now. Served him right, too, but he wasn't entirely repentant. She was even better than he'd remembered, and with a little luck and a lot of charm, he'd have her right where he wanted her—if he didn't die first. Given the way he was feeling at the moment, he found he couldn't rule out the possibility with his usual confidence, but he wouldn't think about that now.

It was really cold on that tile floor, cold enough that he risked more pain in order to spread Red's towel over himself. She hadn't had time to dry off with it, so it was only a little damp and made adequate cover, but the cold was coming up from the floor. His teeth began to chatter, but a short while later he realized that the chill was actually helping his aching ribs. Now if it would just stop the burning in his thigh and the pounding between his ears. More disturbing, he could feel blood pooling beneath his leg. Surely he hadn't ripped open the artery again, not with a silly little fall. He hoped Frankie didn't come in while he was lying here like this. He hoped there were no stains left behind. He hoped Red would feel unbearably sorry for him.

As if on cue, she appeared in blue jeans, tennis shoes and a sweater. Her hair had been pulled back in a low, loose ponytail that did nothing to tame it. He found that he was glad for that. He was going to dream about that hair and everything that went with it. Perverse devil that he was, he loved this opening period of infatuation. It was in some ways more fun than the chase, only surpassed, in fact, by the first heady period of possession. Everything, as he well knew, went downhill from there if pushed any length of time. In general, he preferred to get out before fascination turned to disappointment and, too often, general disgust. Something hinted that the game could be spun out for some time in this case, and that made him vaguely uncomfortable, but he pushed the feeling aside. His plate was already full with unwanted complications and hindrances. He saw that she had a thick white terry-cloth robe draped over one arm.

"This won't fit," she said, stepping into the room and going down on one knee, "but it'll have to do."

He shook his head gingerly. "I'll just get blood on that. I have some things around here somewhere. They used to be upstairs in the bedroom closet. Frankie might have packed them away to make room. The attic maybe, or—"

"Hold on." She got up and left, taking the robe with her.

He heard her rummaging around in Frank's bedroom. Pretty cheeky of her, as far as he was concerned, but he didn't have the least notion what was going on around here, and he hurt too badly to really care at the moment. She came back with an old flannel robe of his and a pair of pajamas he had never worn and never intended to.

"Better?"

"Forget the pajamas."

"Those are for later, when you leave the hospital."

"I won't be staying in the hospital."

"We'll see."

The doorbell rang. She dropped the robe in his lap, stacked the pajamas on the toilet lid and left him. She returned moments later with two uniformed men. One of them he recognized.

"Hey, Griff! What's up, buddy?"

He smiled weakly. "Good to see you, Todd. Bull got me in the first round of the finals. I think I've busted some stitches. Leg's bleeding, but I don't think I've opened the artery again." He was aware of Red frowning in the doorway, arms folded.

Todd stepped into the small room, medical kit in tow, and crouched down. "Let's take a look." He reached for the towel, and Red abruptly disappeared. "Heard about the accident," he went on conversationally. "Some folks saw it on TV, but I was on duty that day." He worked efficiently and quickly as he spoke, then fell silent. After a few moments, he dictated his findings to his partner. "Pressure slightly elevated. Temp's 101.2. Besides the leg wound, we've got three or four broken ribs and a sprained right wrist. I'm guessing the sling's to keep pressure off a broken clavicle, too." He looked at Griff questioningly, and Griff nodded. "Anything else I should know about? Hit your head when you fell?" Griff lifted his eyebrows, a shrug being too painful. Todd flicked a light in his eyes and looked at his partner. "Possible concussion. Get the stretcher, and ask Joan to come in."

Joan. Griff sighed with satisfaction. He'd been wondering about that. She reappeared almost instantly, arms still folded, face impassive. Was she wondering if he was going to tell of her part in his latest "accident"? He managed a smug smile despite the throbbing pain. She ignored him pointedly.

"Do you know what medications he's taking and where they are?" Todd asked. She answered in the affirmative, bringing a lift to Griff's eyebrows, and went to get them. Todd applied compression to the bleeding wound while she was gone and made chitchat. "When was the last time I saw you? Must've been six, seven years. Tough way to make a living, bud, but you always were one for excitement." The moment she returned, he took the pill bottles in hand, inquired as to the most recent ingestion, noted the time on the bottles themselves and zipped them into a plastic bag, which he duly labeled.

"You should know that he showed up here last night with a snoot full of whiskey, too," Joan said, her glare daring him to deny it.

Todd clucked his tongue, while making notations on the bag. "Griff, Griff, Griff. That's bad stuff, mixing dope like this with alcohol. You got a death wish, boy?"

"Nope, just a bad ache and some questionable friends."

"Well, we'll take care of the ache," Todd said. "The friends you'll have to manage on your own."

"I'll remember that."

Todd dropped the plastic bag on Griff's abdomen and said conversationally, "I assume you've gotten ahold of Frankie in Florida."

Griff was stunned but managed to cover his shock with a brilliant "Uhhh."

Joan shot him an enigmatic look and shifted in the doorway. "Not yet. It—it was late when he came in last night. I—I haven't had a chance this morning."

Todd was closing up his bag. His partner clattered into the bedroom with a gurney and basket. "If you want, I'll give her a call."

"No!"

Joan tossed Griff a look that was part surprise, part suspicion. "Why not, may I ask?"

Griff mentally scrambled for a plausible reason, and as usual, inspiration struck. "I—I want to talk to her myself," he said grandly. "That way she'll know I'm going to be all right." He slid a glance at Joan. Her eyes were narrowed, lashes glinting copper in the light, mouth turning down at the corners. She muttered something about getting out of the way and disappeared. He breathed a silent *whew!*

At Griff's insistence, Todd helped him into the flannel robe and onto the basket, a long, reinforced wire stretcher shaped like half of a hot-dog bun. Together Todd and his partner carried Griff from the bathroom and strapped him, stretcher and all, to the gurney. They threw a blanket over him and wheeled him out into the hallway. Joan was zipping Danna into a pink car coat with a hood lined in white artificial fur, her own navy wool jacket thrown over one shoulder. Danna stooped and picked up something as the gurney drew near. The paramedics stopped, and she went up on tiptoe.

"Here's the paper, Mr. Shaw," she said softly, her big eyes sad. "Does it hurt real bad?"

He managed a smile and smoothed a hand over the back of her head. "Don't worry about me, darlin'. I'm too tough to hurt very bad. I'll see you later."

Todd looked a question at Joan. "You can ride with him if you want."

She shook her head. "We'll follow in the car. I have the feeling we'll be coming back without Mr. Shaw."

Griff closed his eyes, suddenly weary, and felt the throbbing in his head and thigh, the aches throughout his body, but he was thinking that he'd be back soon enough, sooner than Joan might think. He didn't know what Frankie was doing in Florida or when she'd be back, but he knew that he'd stumbled into a sweet setup here, and he didn't intend to give it up so lightly. He had to stay someplace after all, and a hospital wasn't his style. Besides, this was his house. Well, Frankie's name was on the title, but he had bought and paid for the place—and gladly, if it came to that. He knew that his grandmother would want him here right now, and that she'd probably come running if she should find out that he was hurt, which was why he didn't intend to tell her, at least not for some time.

He wondered how soon he could convince Joan to play house and how long he would want it to go on—surely until the end of his convalescence. Anything else would be decidedly awkward unless he moved elsewhere, which wasn't out of the question. But he wouldn't think of that now. Too much forethought often ruined the enjoyment, removed the spontaneity, occasionally even sparked his conscience to life, and he had found that an active conscience was often a killjoy, almost as much an obstruction to a good time as serious pain, the kind of pain he was feeling now.

He tried to concentrate on the game afoot, plotting his next step in the seduction of Joan, the luscious redhead, though acutely aware of every jiggle and jar of the gurney as Todd and Partner maneuvered him out the front door and down the steps to the walk below and the ambulance waiting at the curb. He didn't tell himself how foolish he had been to walk in on her while in this condition, and he didn't entertain the idea that his ambitions where the fiery redhead was concerned might not be realized. He was like the Canadian Mounties after all; he always got his woman. It just never occurred to him that Joan might be the one woman in the world for whom his heralded attractions held more terror than charm.

Chapter Three

She steeled herself with a deep breath and fresh resolve, even while she couldn't help wishing that his injuries were less—or more—serious. Incongruous as it seemed, the notion made perfect sense. Had he been less seriously hurt, she could and would have set him out on the street before dark, and had his injuries been only slightly more serious, the doctor would not have allowed Griff Shaw to browbeat him into letting him leave the hospital in the morning.

As it was, she supposed he would of necessity be her concern for a day or two more. Surely it wouldn't take longer than that to find somewhere else to go. She might even be able to find someone in this town who would be thrilled to give a clean bed to the famous Griff Shaw, but she couldn't really see herself doing that. It was his house after all. He ought to be able to recuperate there with his grandmother to tend him, but that, too, would take some time to arrange. Meanwhile, it might be prudent to begin as she meant to go on. That decided, she pushed through the heavy hospital door and walked briskly into the room.

He opened one eye as she drew near the foot of the bed, then beamed her a thousand-watt smile, and fixed her with benign attention. She opened her mouth to speak, but he beat her to it. "Where's the princess?"

It did not compute. She folded her arms. "I beg your pardon?"

"Danna," he said helpfully. "She's a real little darlin', thanks no doubt to your good raisin' and sweet temperament. I was just wondering where she is?"

Joan had to smile. He might be too handsome to live, but he wasn't very smart if he thought he could get on her good side by pandering to her obvious concern for and pride in her daughter. "Danna's fine, thank you very much. I ran her over to my sister's while you were asleep. But I'm not concerned about Danna just now. How do you feel, Mr. Shaw?"

He let that blinding smile fade to a dim glow. "I'm not one to complain, ma'am, but that old bull sure did a job on me. I didn't realize how banged up I am till this morning's fall."

She nodded smartly, not buying it for a minute. Oh, he was injured all right, seriously, but she knew the sort of man he was. Whether or not he'd known before he'd opened the door that she was in the bathtub, he would use the incident to his advantage if she allowed it. Not that she didn't feel a twinge of guilt about her part in bursting open his stitches. Her temper. Sometimes it just got the best of her. Still, he could've saved them both a lot of misery and inconvenience if he'd just stayed on that couch, and she meant to make him understand that.

"About this morning, Mr. Shaw," she began.

"Call me Griff," he interjected smoothly, ignoring her look of irritation.

"About this morning, Griff," she began again, but he went on as if she hadn't spoken.

"I know we haven't been properly introduced, but you obviously knew who I was when you put me to bed on your couch last night, and I did hear Todd refer to you as Joan." He paused, grinning, as if to say it was her turn now.

She knew this game. The object was to control the conversation and elicit the replies he wanted to hear, replies he would use against her later when she balked at his suggestions. Well, she wouldn't play. She put her hands on her hips and waited, certain he would say more, take another shot, so to speak. He didn't disappoint her. After an awkward moment, he rubbed a spot on his shoulder, just above his broken collarbone. It was a masterful move intended to remind her of his injuries and imply helplessness. But she knew instinctively that this man was about as helpless as an adder.

"Anybody ever call you Jo?"

She disciplined a smile. "On occasion."

"I imagine it sits more kindly than Red."

"Depends," she said, striking a bored pose.

"On what?"

"On who's calling and why."

"Ah." His blue eyes sparkled. "Well, what's it to be then, Red or Jo?"

She smiled, knowing she had him dead to rights, and sauntered closer to the bed. "Just so we understand one another, *Griff,*" she said sweetly but with growing coldness, "I couldn't care less what you call me, and yes, I knew who you were when I let you sleep on the couch last night. Otherwise I'd have put you out with the other two. And if you ever open a door on me again, you'll be needing stitches in brand-new places as well as another ambulance. Count on it." She knew by the fleeting look of shock on his face that she'd made her point. He even had the grace to color slightly, but she didn't want to hear any phony explanations or long-winded apologies, so she turned her back to him and hurried on. "Now, we have to make some decisions. I understand that you have no hospitalization insurance. Given what you do for a living, I'm not surprised. The question is, then, can you afford a lengthy stay in the hospital?"

He snorted. "Can anybody?"

She grimaced, then composed herself and turned back to face him. "Then I'll have to call your grandmother and ask her to come home."

He opened his mouth as if to protest, then closed it again and seemed to consider before slowly shaking his head. "I hate to bother her. Only God knows when she last vacationed like this."

Oh, he was good, very, very good. She, too, hated to interrupt Frankie's stay in Florida—for more than Frankie's sake—as he must well know. But what must be done, must be done. She shrugged. "Frankie would want to know at any rate, and you should be able to stay in your own home. Danna and I will simply have to find some other place to live."

"Now that's plain silly," he argued. "Frankie wanted you in the house or she wouldn't have left you there, and I certainly don't want to put you out. Besides, I don't think I could manage on my own just now. We could always—"

"No." She had learned long ago that a single word often left no room for argument, but she could see that he was going to try. She turned her back on him again, saying, "I'll call her tonight."

"I really think I ought to do that," he said, but she shook her head.

"Frankie's no hothouse flower. Besides, she knows and trusts me." *And I couldn't trust you to talk to her,* she added silently. "I'll give her this number, so she can call you if she wants."

He looked perfectly disgusted. "Couldn't we talk about this?" he said, bringing up his good knee and resting his forearm on it.

She smiled faintly. "Nothing to talk about. You need care. I can't give it to you. Frankie can."

"But where will you go?"

"Don't concern yourself about that."

"I don't want you to leave!"

She managed not to laugh. "I'm aware of that."

"But..."

Temper flared again, but she tamped it down, wielding the icy control she had developed by way of self-preservation. "It isn't going to do you any good, you know," she said bitingly. "I know your type. In fact, I already know your line. One glimpse and you've suddenly developed a raging passion for me, a passion, of course, which you're completely unable to control—until it comes time to leave, that is. By that time, you'll be totally cured. Well, take the cure now, cowboy, and save yourself the bother. I'm immune, inoculated by experience." The look on his face produced chuckles, if not humor. She almost felt sorry for him. Almost. She reached for the door, tossing him a cryptic look over her shoulder. "Sleep well, Mr. Shaw. The doctor says you need it."

She walked out into the hallway, satisfied that she'd effectively spiked his guns, for the time being anyway, long enough for Frankie to get here. But then what? She'd already had a look at the newspaper, and not a single new listing had been printed in the rentals column. Maybe tomorrow or Sunday.

And there was always Amy. True, it wouldn't be comfortable, but they could make do for a while if they had to. One way or another, she would not be trapped in close quarters any longer than absolutely necessary with the likes of Griff Shaw. His brand of trouble she did not need. Once had been enough for her. More than enough.

She put Danna to bed with the usual routine. A bath. A snack. Toothbrushing. Hair brushing. A prayer. A song. A kiss. And sometimes a little conversation. Tonight the topic had been chosen in order to prepare her young daughter for yet another move. How, Joan had asked, would she like to visit Aunt Amy for a while? Danna had screwed up her face and said nothing.

Joan understood. It wasn't that Danna didn't love her aunt, but Amy smoked too much and seldom bothered to clean her place, so the stale odor permeated everything. Besides, Amy was not a happy woman. Childless by her own choice, she had lost her husband two years ago after a long illness. He had left her secure financially, but in some ways that only made it worse, for Amy had no drive, no need to do anything but sit and smoke and grieve. She was only thirty-six, older than Joan by some seven years, but not too old to make something of her life if only she would.

But it was an old battle, and one Joan had no wish to fight again. She was just too tired for it and had too many problems of her own. Amy was not the only one to have loved and lost after all. Amy was not the only one to grieve and hurt. Joan couldn't help thinking, though, how ironic it was that Amy, who had no one but herself, should be financially solvent, while she struggled to raise her daughter on a beginning teacher's salary. Yet it was Danna who made all the difference in her own life. It was for Danna that she got up in the mornings and for Danna that she spent her nights tidying up and sewing and plotting ways to meet the newest financial disaster head-on. For Danna's sake, she would do anything, even put up with Griff Shaw, if it came to that. But it wouldn't. Frankie would come. Griff, after all, was Frankie's Danna.

How strange to think of him that way, not that she wanted to think of him at all. She didn't, of course. Why would she? He was trouble, that one, too attractive by half and all too aware of it. Thought himself irresistible. Well, not to her. She had learned the hard way that men like Griff Shaw came guaranteed with heartache. Even Frankie must worry on that account, for he would never do the safe or the reasonable thing. He craved danger and would always perform his best when failure loomed largest. It was part of his charm, an addendum to the overweening ego of a man with more sex drive than scruples. Poor Frankie, but better Frankie than her.

She went downstairs and settled into the armchair. Tiny colored lights winked at her through the dark needles of the cedar tree she and Danna had cut from a friend's pasture. They could not afford to purchase a tree, and this one was far from perfect, but it was better in its way. She would never forget how Danna had laughed and squealed as they'd sawed away at the trunk or how her tongue had poked out the side of her mouth as she'd struggled to help haul the fallen tree to the car. She would never forget how they'd carefully unwrapped the delicate glass bulbs and hung them on the tree. Later, she'd had to rearrange them, for all those Danna had hung were clustered at her own eye level near the bottom, but the fun had been in the doing, not necessarily in the final result, just as with the popcorn rope they'd strung. Danna had giggled and popped kernels into her mouth whenever she thought Joan was not looking, and Joan had looked away a lot on purpose. It had taken nights and nights to complete barely ten feet of the thing, but they had done it together, and that was all that mattered. Now they would have to leave the tree behind. It would never survive the move.

But they would have another. They'd cut another. They'd decorate another. There was time before Christmas. But what of Christmas? She had bought very few presents. Most of Danna's were still on layaway. How would she ever manage Christmas and the move, too? They would have to go to Amy's, at least until after the holidays and she could gather together additional funds. It would be awkward, but it would be okay. They'd survived worse.

She shivered, remembering those eight awful days they'd slept in the car. After he'd left them. After the money had run out. She should have called her parents to come for them sooner, but she'd been so determined to make it on her own. It had been her mistake. *He* had been her mistake. Why should anyone else have to pay for it? But then she'd realized that she was making Danna pay, even though Danna had been too small to understand how desperate the situation had become.

Since then, she had worked so hard. She had finished her degree. She had made them a home, *several* homes. She would do it again. It was inevitable anyway. But not this soon. They had only been here since Thanksgiving, but they would have stayed until next summer. By that time she'd have had the cash together to rent them another place of their own and perhaps even partially furnish it. It was that prospect which had made Frankie's house-sitting scheme seem so perfect. Her disappointment was keen.

Besides, she was too tired to move again before Christmas.

For a moment she allowed herself the self-pity of tears. For a moment she heard herself asking God why. But then she closed her eyes and prayed again for strength, and it came. It always came. Sighing thankfully, she reached for the phone and picked up the address book next to it. She found the number and punched it out on the keypad. Two rings later, an elderly voice—not Frankie's—greeted her.

"Hello, this is Joan Burton calling from Duncan, Oklahoma. Could I speak to Frankie Thom please?"

A pause followed. Then the voice told her that Frankie was not there. "I tried to call you earlier, Ms. Burton," the elderly woman said. "I was afraid to try this late. I know you have a little girl. Frankie says she's an angel. I didn't want to chance waking her."

Joan gripped the phone with both hands. "Is something wrong with Frankie?"

"She's had an accident," the woman said. "It was the silliest thing. A duck. We were walking along the boardwalk in the park, and a duck shot out of the grass and attacked Frankie's ankle! A duck, for pity's sake!"

"Is—is Frankie all right?"

"She will be," the woman assured her. "She was stunned. She stumbled and she fell. Hard. The fall broke her hip."

Joan closed her eyes. "Oh, no!"

"She'll be all right," the woman said quickly, "but it will take some time. A few more days in the hospital, and then she can come back here. Six to eight weeks after that, she'll be up and about."

Six to eight weeks. Joan moaned aloud. She couldn't help it. Six to eight weeks. *Oh, God,* she thought, *how could this happen? How could You let this happen?* The woman was speaking, telling her not to worry, that Frankie would be well taken care of, that it was better it had happened there than anywhere else, something about the doctors all practicing geriatrics and nursing services at retirement villages. She could not make herself pay close attention but finally became aware that the woman had paused.

"T-tell Frankie that we'll be praying for her," she said thickly. "Tell her not to worry...about anything, and...we hope she's better soon."

The woman thanked her and said something about contacting Griff.

"I'll take care of that," Joan promised. "I know how to contact him just now. I—I'll have him call her."

She took down the hospital number, thanked the woman, a Mrs. Elliot, and hung up. Oh, Lord, what was she to do now? What could she do but make up the downstairs bedroom for Griff Shaw and bring him back to it from the hospital tomorrow morning? She could not have told Frankie about his injuries now. She didn't need that on top of a broken hip. Perhaps Griff would disagree with her, but if so, he could be the one to tell Frankie his news. She might take it better coming from him. At least she would know that he was well enough to speak for himself. Meanwhile, Joan would have to resign herself to staying here with him for a time. It was not a notion to which she could give in with any grace, but she would do what she must, as usual.

First, however, she was going to investigate the alternatives. There had to be someone, some way... The Reverend Mr. Charles would know. She grasped at that straw with desperate determination. He would understand her dilemma, and he would help her find a solution. Yes, she would call the minister before she did anything else. Some of her panic subsided, and she found herself breathing a little easier. It would be all right. Maybe she and Danna could even stay here. Maybe.

She got up and switched on the television, unwilling to worry or to wonder anymore.

* * *

She came awake hours later, her face burning with remembered passion. It was an old dream, one that had haunted her for months after she'd discovered Dan's first infidelity. In the way of dreams, she was first alone, and then he was there, falling on his knees, tears streaming down his face, begging her forgiveness. He was a broken man, so afraid of losing her that he was trembling, so ashamed that he could not meet her gaze.

"Let me make love to you," he pleaded. "Not sex. I'm not talking about sex. I know the difference now. I can prove that I love you."

And he did. In her dream, he did.

But not in reality. In reality he had told her to "grow up," to "get with the picture." No one was monogamous anymore. She was causing herself needless pain. "It was only sex," he had said, "only sex."

He had never begged, but she had forgiven him anyway, believing that marriage was truly meant to be forever, that love really could conquer all, that he might learn from her example. She had forgiven him, and he had thrown it back in her face. He had found a woman who could "give him more," a woman who "knew the score" and wouldn't try to change him, a woman with money. He called it "an honest exchange," and when she'd asked him what arrangements he meant to make for their daughter, he had merely shaken his head.

"You don't really want me underfoot," he had said, "and it isn't as if she's old enough to remember me once I'm gone." He had told her with thinly veiled disdain that she was parent enough for both of them. "More mother," he had said, "than woman."

And she had taken that last stinging barb into the lonely night with her. Perhaps that was why she continually dreamed that he humbled himself and begged her forgiveness, why she imagined a passion born of love, why she could not risk herself again. Only a fool would put herself through that again. Only a fool would surrender to such intimacies, give herself up in the hope of love. There were safer, truer loves, and she had found that motherhood was one of them. She was a good mother. That was enough. It had to be enough.

She turned off the television and the lights and climbed the stairs. She was standing alone in the dark, her hand reaching for the doorknob to her room, when it came to her that the man in her dream had not been Daniel. The man in her dream had been Griff Shaw.

"Please, Reverend Charles, I didn't know who else to turn to. He's really quite seriously injured. He'll have to stay off that leg, and the ribs are going to pain him for some time, and there's the concussion and the broken collarbone, some sprains. He'll have to have attention, but with Frankie in the shape she's in... Well, there is no one else, and I simply can't do it. I have to work. You know I have to work."

He nodded in understanding and turned an inquiring gaze upon his wife. She was the perfect complement for his dark, smooth, athletic good looks. A dainty blonde, she was very pregnant and miserable with it. Her ankles were swollen and her breathing labored, as if the baby crowded her lungs. Joan remembered the feeling with a mixture of nostalgia and relief, but for her it had only been the last days, not the months Clarice Charles had endured, and yet she smiled, her love for her husband so obvious that it made Joan uncomfortable.

"I couldn't care for him myself," she said, "but perhaps one of the retired ladies in the church or an older couple?"

Bolton Charles nodded doubtfully. "It's the timing of the thing," he said. "So many people will be traveling or having company for the holidays."

"But there must be someone," Mrs. Charles said helpfully.

"Don't worry." Her husband echoed his wife's optimistic tone. "We'll see what we can do, Joan. We have today and tomorrow. I'll make a plea from the pulpit if you like."

Joan mulled that over. Did she want the minister announcing in front of the whole congregation that Griff Shaw was sharing a roof with her and her daughter? It would, of course, be the fastest, surest way to locate anyone interested in taking care of the famous bull rider, but the idea of everyone knowing she was for all intents and purposes, living here alone with him, made the heat rise to her cheeks. She shook her head.

"I'd rather handle this quietly," she said weakly, relieved when the minister nodded understandingly.

"It might be best," he said. "A man like Griff Shaw is bound to have more than his share of pride."

Joan was shocked. He wasn't concerned about her or her reputation at all. It was Griff's! How like a man!

The minister went on speaking. "I'll make a list of everyone who might have room for him, see what they're doing for the holidays and go from there. If that doesn't produce anyone, I'll come over myself and sit with him on Monday so you can go on to work."

She didn't want someone to sit with him. She wanted someone to take him off her hands, but she couldn't say that. They had already praised her for her charity, for her understanding. It seemed not to matter that he, a single man, and she, a single woman, would be living under the same roof, but they couldn't know how dangerous he was, even injured. How could they know, these two good people? She tried to make her point another way.

"What if Mrs. Charles needs you? The baby could come anytime. You have to be available."

He smiled benignly. "My secretary would pinch-hit for me. If truth be told, I was considering asking her to do it anyway."

Joan swallowed and pressed for a little more. "Might she have room for him? Would she consider . . . ?"

He reached forward and patted her hand encouragingly. "We'll see. Meanwhile, you could check the service agencies. They're mostly geared toward the elderly. I doubt he could qualify for aid, but it won't hurt to ask."

"It will have to be Monday, though," Mrs. Charles said apologetically. "They keep office hours like everyone else, I'm afraid."

"At the very least," her husband said, "we'll get somebody in here to help you out so you can work."

Joan nodded numbly. It wasn't enough, but what could she say? They just didn't seem to see the desperate spot she was in. Why didn't they understand that she needed to be free of him? She must be free of him. It wasn't fair. She made herself smile and offer more decaffeinated coffee, but Mrs. Charles shook her head.

"Not for me, thank you. I really must get home and put these horrid feet up, but I have a suggestion." She looked at her husband. "She'll need help getting him home."

He caught her meaning immediately. "Oh, of course. I'll just take Clarice home and meet you at the hospital later. About eleven?"

Joan nodded. How ironic. She wanted him to take Griff Shaw off her hands, not help her bring him here! But they were doing the best they could, she knew, and she was grateful. She expressed that gratitude as best she could as she walked them to the door.

"Just part of the job," the minister said, helping his wife on with her coat. "I hope you know that if things were different right now, we wouldn't hesitate to take him in any more than you have."

If only you knew, she thought, but she managed to say something appropriate. He took her hand and pressed it reassuringly.

"Everything will work out. One has to wonder sometimes why God allows these situations to arise, but rest assured, He knows what He's about."

Joan tried to squelch her feelings of bitterness with a smile and a nod.

"I'm so sorry to hear about Frankie," Mrs. Charles said. "Send her our love when next you speak to her."

"And tell her she'll be in our prayers," the reverend added. "All of you will be in our prayers."

We'll need them, she thought and sent them on their way.

The next hour was spent making preparations to drop off Danna at Amy's, then putting clean sheets on Frankie's bed and clean towels in the bathroom. She was going to miss that tub, she thought resentfully. But perhaps it wouldn't be for long. Perhaps some kind soul would come forward and save her from living under the same roof with Griff Shaw. And perhaps some long-lost treasure would turn up with her name engraved on it. She turned off the self-pity and got Danna into her coat before hustling her into the car.

It would work out, she told herself as she backed her old station wagon out of the garage. Maybe she could talk Amy into taking him in. Maybe, in fact, he was just what Amy needed—someone to focus on besides herself. His presence would certainly give purpose to her life. She wondered why she hadn't thought of it before, but after ten minutes with Amy in her cluttered kitchen, Joan knew it was a lost cause.

"I've done my share of nursing, thank you," she said, pausing to take a long drag on her cigarette. She blew out the smoke, then ran a hand carelessly through her short brown hair. "I wouldn't put myself through that again for anything."

"But, Amy, you have the room, and you don't work."

"No way. Besides, didn't I tell you? I'm going up to the city tomorrow. Mom wants me to help her finish her Christmas shopping. The folks will want to know what you've decided about the holiday. Should I tell them you're coming?"

Joan sighed. "I don't know. If I'm going to have to babysit Griff Shaw, I don't see how I can."

"They're going to be awfully disappointed," Amy reminded her, "Danna being the only grandbaby."

Joan put a hand to her head. It was pounding. Stress, she assumed. "I'll try. Tell them I'll try. But Amy, won't you reconsider? If you could take him just for a few days."

Amy got up from the table and walked to the sink, shaking her head. She was putting on weight, letting herself go, Joan noticed. She felt a stab of fear for her sister and a deep sense of disappointment.

"Just tell him to get out," Amy was saying.

Joan shook her head. "I can't do that, not without giving him someplace else to go. I mean, it's his house, for Pete's sake, and he's hurt."

"That was always your problem. You just couldn't say no. You bought every sob story that came your way. All those Sunday school lessons, I guess."

"You had the same lessons," Joan reminded her softly.

"There haven't been any Sunday school lessons since Mark died," Amy said flatly, "and there won't be."

Joan bit her lip, trapping her tongue in her mouth. She'd tried preaching, but Amy's bitterness was so deep she just couldn't get through it. At least she hadn't lost the very will to live as Amy had. At least she hadn't lost faith. At least she had Danna. She knew it was useless to preach, but maybe a suggestion...

She traced a coffee stain on the tablecloth with her forefinger. "You know, I really like that minister, Reverend Bolton Charles. He has this quiet strength, this...I don't know, confidence...something. I understand that he's quite a good counselor, too."

Amy smirked at her. "Coming on a bit strong, little sister. I don't need a counselor."

"You need something, Amy," Joan told her gently.

Amy shrugged. "What I need died a long time ago. Now shouldn't you be going?"

"I worry about you, Amy."

"Don't. You've got enough to worry about, and there's nothing to be done for me."

Sighing, Joan got up from her chair. Amy reached for another cigarette. "I should have him settled in by noon," she said, deliberately brightening her voice. "I'll give you lunch when you bring Danna over."

Amy shook her head, sucking nicotine. "I'll get something here. You'll have your hands full with that cowboy."

Defeated, Joan nodded and buttoned her coat. "Thanks for watching Danna."

Amy just jerked her head at the door. "Your cowboy's waiting."

Not my cowboy, Joan corrected her silently. *Never my cowboy.*

One thing seemed clear to Joan. Amy's determination to hold off everyone and everything that might reawaken her emotions seemed to have grown greater over the two years since her husband's death. Joan sometimes despaired of ever again enjoying the bright, sparkling sister she had once known. Amy had been so very supportive of her immediately after Dan had left, offering to fly out to California to be with her and Danna. Only pride had kept Joan from accepting that offer. She had half believed that moving to Duncan to be near Amy would somehow benefit them both, but it seemed as if Amy refused to emotionally acknowledge her existence. At least she had Danna, while Amy had no one. No one.

Chapter Four

They were laughing in there! The dissolute cowboy and the preacher, laughing like old friends. She slapped a sandwich onto the plate and grabbed a cup from the cabinet for the tomato soup. What was wrong with the reverend? Couldn't he tell what sort of man Griff Shaw was? Did the charm oozing from those manly pores so obscure the nature beneath to everyone but her? She shook her head, disgusted to the soles of her feet, and spread crackers around the edge of the plate. He was going to eat her out of house and home. She knew it.

The doorbell rang just as she lifted the tray, but an instant later she heard it open and the patter of little feet. Danna came running down the hall, her mittens hanging by strings from her sleeves, her cap perched on the crown of her head instead of covering her ears. "Is he here?" she demanded breathlessly.

Joan nodded, frowning. "Where's Amy?"

"Right here." She appeared behind Danna, her own coat thrown on haphazardly, a cigarette burning between her fingers.

Joan tamped down her temper. "Amy, you know you can't smoke in here."

Amy rolled her eyes. "And who's going to tell the old woman?"

"Well, her grandson's lying in the bed in the other room, you know."

Amy grimaced. "I'm going anyway." She walked out without another word of goodbye.

Danna shrugged out of her coat and carried it to the chair by the table. "Is he okay?"

"He's still hurt, if that's what you mean, but he's getting better."

"Can he eat?"

"Yes. I'm just taking him his lunch now."

"Can I go?"

"To take him his lunch?"

Danna nodded, her eyes large. Joan stifled a groan. Oh, not Danna, too! Well, she wouldn't have it. She just wouldn't.

"Why don't you wash up? I'll get your lunch for you in a minute."

Danna pulled a long face. "Is he mad?"

"Mad? Why ever would you think that?" Her daughter hitched up a little shoulder. Joan stilled the impulse to roll her eyes as Amy had done before. "No, he isn't mad."

"Why can't I go, then?"

Joan opened her mouth to snap that she just couldn't, then closed it again, calmed herself and capitulated. "All right, you can come, but only for a minute."

Danna wiggled an eyebrow, leaving her mother to wonder what on earth that was about! She turned shy the moment they were through the bedroom door, hanging back and sticking a finger in her mouth. Griff spotted her instantly, looking past the minister, who had drawn up a chair next to his bed. They presented a study in contrasts, the cowboy with his rumpled, dark brown hair, twinkling blue eyes, overnight growth of whiskers and skintight white T-shirt, the minister with his even darker hair, almost black eyes, cleanly shaved jaw and well-tailored suit. Danna seemed not to mind that Griff looked so much the worse for wear, at least not when he smiled at her.

"Hey, gorgeous! Come on in here. Come on."

Danna pranced up right next to the bed, beaming.

"Miss Danna," the Reverend Mr. Charles said. "Nice to see you again."

She gave him a sweet smile and turned her attention back to Griff, propped her elbows on the bed, her chin in her hands.

Griff tapped her on the end of her nose. "You worried about me, sunshine?" She nodded and giggled, leaning her weight into the side of the bed. "Well, don't be," he said. "I'm right fine and getting better all the time." He shot a look at Joan. "May take me a while to get up to full speed," he went on, "but in the meantime, it's sure good of you and your mommy to look after me."

Bolton Charles stood up and offered Danna his chair. "I have to be going," he said and extended his hand to the patient. "Good to meet you, Griff. I look forward to another visit."

"Sure thing. Any old time, and thanks for your help."

"No problem." He glanced at Joan, smiling. "Could I have a word with you?"

"Sure." She bent to place the tray on Griff's lap, remembered his wounded thigh and straightened, then set the tray carefully on the side of the bed. That T-shirt, she noticed, molded to his body in such a way as to reveal every muscle, every plane, every dip and curve of a well-developed chest. "Can you manage this by yourself?" she asked, her tone more curt than she'd intended.

He glanced up and nodded. "I think so."

"I'll look in on you after I get Danna her lunch."

"I want to eat in here, Mommy, with Mr. Shaw," her innocent daughter exclaimed pleadingly.

Joan's dismay must have shown on her face, for Danna quickly bowed her head, and Griff Shaw inserted a fabricated chuckle. "Well, I'm flattered, sweetie," he said, "but I'm pretty done in. How about this? You keep me company until your mommy has your lunch ready, then you can go along to the kitchen and eat there while I catch me a nap." He looked up at Joan. "Deal?"

She didn't like having Griff Shaw negotiate disputes between herself and her daughter, but she was wise enough to know that failure to bend at this moment might cause a break between the two of them later. Reluctantly she nodded her approval and left them to their visit. She ushered the minister from the room and walked with him down the hall to the foyer. "Would you like to sit in the living room?"

He shook his head. "That's not necessary. I just wanted to let you know that a couple of ladies will be coming in next week to tend to your patient during the day so you can work. After that, we'll have to see. If you don't mind my asking, what are your plans for the holidays?"

She sighed and lifted a hand to her temple. "Well, I had hoped we'd find someone else to take him in so we could go to my parents' home in Oklahoma City, but if that's out, I suppose we'll just stay here."

He nodded, his dark eyes shining with compassion. "I know this is difficult for you, and I truly regret that Clarice and I can't do more just now."

"Oh, you've been wonderful," she assured him warmly. "I don't know what I'd have done without you!"

He smiled. "I'm glad if we've helped, and don't hesitate to call on us again anytime. By the way, those two ladies may be carrying in some food from time to time. You know how they are. If somebody's down sick, they think they're honor bound to feed him. I assumed you wouldn't mind, thought it might ease any financial strain."

"Oh, thank you. It'll help. I'll admit that I'm a bit worried."

"Well, don't be. We won't let you shoulder the whole load alone. One good turn, after all, deserves another, and this is a good thing you're doing. Remember that when that outlaw in there tries your patience, will you?"

Her gaze sharpened. How did he know? Then she nodded. "I'll try."

"Good. I'll be talking to you soon."

She nodded, trying not to feel abandoned as he slung on his coat and left her.

It was not a happy woman who spread salad dressing on two pieces of lightly toasted bread and followed it with three thin slices of turkey breast, a crisp leaf of lettuce and a small dill pickle cut lengthwise. She sliced the sandwich on the diagonal and placed half of it on a plate for Danna and half of it on a plate for herself. With the sounds of giggles and laughter grating against her nerves, she reheated the soup and poured it into two cups. Two glasses of milk and a plate of saltines completed the simple meal.

When the table was set, she steeled herself and called her daughter to eat. Several seconds passed before she decided to call again. Barely a heartbeat later, Danna appeared, her eyes large, her expression a mixture of confusion and concern. Joan instantly castigated herself for her temper and sour mood. Determinedly she lightened her expression and put on a smile.

"Well, how was your visit with Aunt Amy?" she asked, pulling out a chair for Danna.

Danna shrugged and promptly switched the subject to the very one Joan would have given several fingers to avoid. "Did you know it was a big old bull took its horn and stabbed it into Griff's leg? Eeew! It was all bloody and yucky! And it kicked him, too, and stepped on him and it threw him over its head, all snorting and big and mean. Ooh!" She shivered and dived into her sandwich with both hands. "Yum."

Joan was dumbfounded. How dare he tell her little girl the gory details of his stupid accident! Danna, however, appeared blithely unaffected. Her little feet swinging, she slurped her soup and munched her sandwich and built a pyramid with her crackers. Joan suppressed her resentment, mumbling unheeded platitudes and needless explanations. "The thing is," she said at last, "that Mr. Shaw got on that bull of his own accord. It's his idea of fun, to take such ridiculous chances."

"No, it's not. It's his job," Danna contradicted smoothly.

Joan was cut to the quick. "H-he doesn't have to do it. He could do something saner, something safer."

Danna shrugged again and requested another pickle.

"There aren't any more," Joan said quietly.

"Okay."

Five minutes later, she wiped her mouth and asked to get down from the table. Joan pulled out her chair and helped her to her feet, then tugged her shirt down and tightened her ponytail. She wanted to let her go without saying anything else, but somehow she just couldn't. "Danna," she said, "I don't think you should call him Griff. Mr. Shaw is more proper."

Danna's expression was openly curious. "How come? He gave his mermission."

"Permission."

"Perpission."

It was such an endearingly childlike mistake that it softened Joan's heart instantly. "All right," she said. "Now run along and play."

Danna skipped off humming to herself. Joan put the dishes in the sink and gathered her resources for another confrontation with Griff Shaw. She would not let him anger her. She would be calm and reasonable and firm, and when she was done, he would understand that her daughter was off-limits for him. She wouldn't have Danna hurt by that man. Period.

Shoulders back and chin high, she strode into the room. He was lying on his side, chasing a cracker crumb around an otherwise empty plate with his fingertip. He dusted his hands off, turned carefully onto his back and propped his upper body against two pillows.

"Truce?" he asked, a sparkle in those blue eyes.

She lifted both brows. "I wasn't aware there was a war."

His mouth twitched. "Aw, come on, Red. We both know you're still mad as hell."

She tamped down the flare of anger that would prove him true and strove mightily for a calm she didn't feel. "I'm terribly sorry if I've given you that impression," she said coolly. "I assure you nothing could be further from the truth. I do have some concerns, however."

He stuck his tongue in his cheek, and she knew very well that he was trying not to smile. "Such as?"

She moved her gaze away from the bed with admirable aplomb. "My first concern, naturally, has to be my daughter. She's only five, you know, and as gullible as any child her age."

"Um. The point being?"

"The point being," she repeated tartly, "I don't want you confusing her... filling her head with... stories and..."

"What *stories* would those be?"

"The gruesome details of your injury, for one," she snapped.

"I didn't notice that she was particularly traumatized," he said lightly.

Joan made an attempt to retain control of her temper. "Let's be frank, shall we?"

"Let's."

"Danna's missed... the influence of a father. She's vulnerable to any man who seems to like her."

"I don't *seem* to like her. I *do* like her."

She fixed him with a doubtful gaze. "But you'll be leaving very soon, and I don't want my daughter heartbroken when you go." She rushed on before he could interrupt. "Save your charm for those foolish females of an age to deliver what you're after."

He was angry. The burn of those blue eyes and the muscle twitching in a set jaw proclaimed it, but she lifted her chin and stood her ground, quite certain she was right in this. Nostrils flaring and hands clenched into fists, he took a deep breath and when he spoke, his tone was deceptively smooth. "It's a good thing," he said, "that I can't get up out of this bed."

She sensed something ominous beneath his even tone but refused to submit to it. "Oh?"

"A very good thing," he went on, "because I'm tempted to shake you until your teeth fall out." Her eyes flew wide in alarm. "But then," he said wryly, "I'd probably just wind up kissing you." Her mouth fell open, and he had the audacity to grin. "You see, I have a temper, too, but I have sense enough to know I'd be better served by the kissing than the shaking, and so, I think, would you."

She gasped, outraged and offended. "Of all the conceited, arrogant things to say!"

He shook his head, the glint of devilment in his blue eyes. "Won't wash, Jo. You're a great deal of woman who's been without a man far too long, and we both know that if you weren't attracted to me, you wouldn't be wringing your hands right now."

She dropped her hands to her sides, color climbing her cheeks. "That's the most absurd thing I've ever heard!"

"Now don't make me prove it," he said.

"You're the very last man I'd want to— I—I thought I made myself clear yesterday. You're exactly the sort of man I *don't* want!"

"Well, that does it!" he said, then threw back the covers and moved toward the side of the bed. The tray of empty dishes on the bedside table rattled warningly.

"What do you think you're doing?" she cried just as he grabbed his thigh and doubled up in pain.

"Oh, not again!" he groaned, tossing his head back in agony.

Joan rushed to his side and bent anxiously over the bed. In the next instant, he slipped his sprained wrist free of the sling and his arms came around her and pulled her down beside him. She was too stunned at first to react when his mouth covered hers, and when reaction came, it came in a wave of hot, liquid longing that stunned her anew. Erotic images from last night's dream flashed before her mind's eye, and her body softened and heated in response. Even as she hated herself for the weakness that she betrayed, she could not prevent certain physical results—a parting of lips, a gentle straining upward, the swelling of various parts of her body. For one moment, for one awful, wonderful moment, her defenses were down and she was utterly female, wholly woman, while some other part of her was plunged into an old, hateful grief for what she could not have. Belatedly she wrenched away from him and rolled to her feet. Her hand swung out, palm open. He caught it, palm to palm, with his own and parted her fingers with his in a tight but painless grip.

"Let go!"

"Wait! Just wait!"

"Let go!"

She tried to pull away from him. He pulled back and hauled her effortlessly onto the bed. She froze, face-to-face with the most frightening, horrifying threat of her existence. Blue eyes plumbed amber ones, then his grip loosened and allowed her to slip free.

"What in hell did he do to you?" he asked softly.

She looked away from the pain reflected on his face, covered her mouth with her hand and ran for her life. She heard him calling her name, but she could not have gone back in there if his had been the very voice of God. Instead she rounded the banister and fled up the stairs to her room, where she paced and pounded pillows until the anger left her with only the remembered torment of a freshly broken heart.

At the sound of the door closing, Griff pushed himself into a sitting position, folded the bed covers neatly at his waist and pasted a smile on his face. She wouldn't come until she had to. He knew that, and he couldn't blame her. He'd looked into her eyes that day and seen a shattered soul and heart. It had kept him awake, that look, and he wasn't surprised that she'd taken the coward's way out, coming to his room only when it could not be avoided, speaking only when she must but never about what he'd done. He'd proven a point, and he'd decided that he wasn't sorry about it, but he did regret that he hadn't gauged, indeed, hadn't even considered, the depth of hurt that he was working against.

He was shocked, actually. He hadn't even known such hurt existed except in the imaginations of overly emotional artistic types. It had shaken him. Worse, it made him wonder how many times he had overlooked just such agony.

Well, he was a pragmatic man. He couldn't undo the past, and he was right about two things anyway. She was the kind of woman who needed a man, and the attraction was very real and very mutual. It could also be very mutually satisfying. Now all he had to do was convince her of that. He hoped a little plain speaking might accomplish what smiles and flirtation had not, but before he could get very far with that thought, Danna poked her head in the doorway.

"Hi!"

"Well, hi, sweetie! My, don't you look pretty."

She preened for him in her dark green jumper and white blouse. The jumper, he noted, was a bit worn in places and a trifle short. The cuff of one sleeve of her blouse was unbuttoned to allow more room for a chubby arm, the hand of which clutched a large, wrinkled sheet of manila paper. The princess needed a new gown. He made a mental note.

"How was school?"

"Fine!"

"Got some artwork there, something to show me?"

Brown eyes sparkling, she nodded and stepped forward, thrusting the paper out in a gesture both eager and shy. He took it and studied it, trying to identify what appeared to be the central figure, a large, roundish unicorn with cotton candy sprouting from its nose. Surely not. He tried another tack. Those were either cacti in the background or...naw, they couldn't be elves, with one arm turned up and another turned down like that. He slid a glance sideways, hoping for some sort of illumination.

"It's a bull!" she said.

A bull! "Well, of course it is," he exclaimed, "and a very good one, too! And look at all those cacti. But what..." He turned the paper slightly, studying two objects at the top of the sheet that resembled a pair of brown bananas with spikes on one end.

Danna giggled. "That's you, silly!" When he raised his eyebrows in inquiry, she went on, her tone indicating that he was a goofball if ever there was one. "Your boots when you was up in the air!"

Realization dawned. "This is a picture of me getting bucked off that old bull!"

She nodded triumphantly, dug her elbows into the edge of the mattress and plopped her chin into her cupped hands. A feeling like none other he'd ever experienced swept over him.

"Did you draw this for me, sugar?"

The sweetest smile curved her mouth. Then she reached out, took the paper and turned it over. There on the back, written awkwardly in faint pencil were the words FOR GRIFF LOVE DANNA.

Love Danna. Suddenly he felt as if a huge wad of that cotton candy was stuck in his throat. It was just a piece of paper, for pity's sake, just a piece of paper with some odd-looking, silly...truly wonderful crayon scribblings. And she'd done it just for him. For him. He had to clear his throat, twice, before he could speak again. "This is really something. I...I'll treasure it always. It's...almost as wonderful as you." He leaned over and wrapped his good arm around her. Her little arms went around his neck. She hugged him gingerly as if afraid he might break. He closed his eyes, feeling such...*love?* He whispered, "Thanks, honey."

She sat back and looked at him with intense satisfaction, as if giving him this funny drawing had made her unspeakably happy, as if that careful hug had somehow filled a need in her. He felt deeply humbled and perilously close to tears. He tried to banish them with winks and smiles while searching for something clever to say that would help him regain his balance. In the end, it was she who saved him.

"Matt Watson called me a liar today."

Anger flashed through him. "Who the devil's Matt Watson and why would he do such a thing?"

She shrugged and answered in reverse order. "Kevin's big brother."

"Who's Kevin?"

"Boy in my class."

"And just why did Kevin's big brother, Matt, call you a liar?"

"'Cause I said you was here."

Griff narrowed his eyes. "You happen to know his phone number?"

Surprised, she shook her head.

"What's his daddy's name?"

"Wish."

"Holy cow, not old *Wish* Watson?" He laughed and reached for the phone that sat on the corner of the increasingly cluttered bedside table. He punched in the number for directory assistance. "Yes, ma'am. I'd like the telephone number of Shelley Watson, please." He covered the mouth with his hand and said quietly to Danna, "That's his real name, see. Me and old Shelley, we went to school together once upon a time, and he was always whining about how he wished his momma hadn't given him a girl's name. It isn't, but it sounds like one." He paused to listen to the number, repeated it silently to himself and disconnected. "Anyway, we took to calling him Wish, and I guess he liked it better than Shelley, so he kept it." He started punching in the number.

"What are you gonna do?" Danna asked, suddenly alarmed.

He winked at her. "Nothing much. But Matt Watson won't be calling you a liar anymore. Hello! Who's this?" He winked at Danna again. "Well, hello, Matt. This is Griff Shaw. Say, is Wish there? Napping, huh?" He grinned. "Yeah, haul him out."

Danna put her hand over her mouth and giggled. The seconds seemed to drag out, and as they did, Danna's eyes grew larger. He reached out and chucked her under the chin, feeling pretty smug. When the sleepy voice of his old school chum mumbled into the phone, Griff crossed his legs at the ankle and leaned back against his pillows, enjoying himself.

"Hey, Wish. Griff Shaw here. How's it going, old man?" He laughed and listened, watching Danna's face. "Oh, I'm vegetating these days. Bull gored me at the finals, so I'm home recuperating. Nothing much to speak of. Be off my feet awhile. Anyway, my little friend, Danna Burton, tells me she goes to school with your boys, and I was thinking maybe you could bring them over for a visit." She squeaked in surprise and slapped a hand over her mouth. Griff grinned and winked again. "No, no trouble at all. Fact is, I'm bored out of my skull 'bout half the time, and little Danna would sure like it. Okay, sounds great. We'll be expecting you tomorrow afternoon. Oh, he does?"

Danna gave his shirtsleeve a yank, whispering, "What?"

He put his hand over the mouth and whispered back, "Matt's a rodeo fan. Seems he knows my name."

She waggled her shoulders from side to side, saying flatly, "Ever'body round here knows your name. You're a..." Her forehead creased as she tried to remember the term.

"Hometown boy?" he supplied helpfully.

The crease smoothed out. "Yep! A hometown boy!"

He laughed but cut it off as Wish pulled him back to the conversation. "What? Oh? Well, that's all right, Wish. You come on this evening then. Sure. Say about seven? Right. Looking forward to it." He disconnected, set aside the phone and folded his arms, grinning widely.

Danna clapped her hands. "Boy, that old Matt won't call me a liar no more!"

Griff pretended outrage. "The nerve of that kid, calling my Danna a liar!"

The hooting laughter stopped, and in that instant before she wrapped her arms around his neck again, his own words echoed through his mind. *My Danna.* He knew suddenly why Joan was frightened for her daughter, what power he held to hurt this little one. She had lost her father and who knew how many others since. Already she had adopted him. Was it fair to develop this relationship further, only to abandon her again in the end? He closed his eyes, seeing more than he'd wanted to.

He *had* attempted to use her to win over her mother. But he did *like* this little fairy. Like? No, it was more than that. She got to him, this kid, on some elemental level that none other ever had. And he could hurt her.

Well, he wouldn't. That was all there was to it. He simply would not allow himself to hurt this child. He didn't know how he could stop it, what he would do; he only knew that he couldn't bear the thought of causing her pain. And he wanted suddenly to get his hands around Dan Burton's throat. What was wrong with that guy anyway? Leaving behind a kid like this without a second thought. How was it possible. If she were his, *really* his . . .

But no, he wasn't going to start thinking like that. He'd do something really stupid if he started thinking like that. Nope. Best to let things develop another way. What she needed was a friend, a grown-up friend, someone she could relate to and giggle with.

Keep it light, he told himself as she wiggled free and those brown eyes danced at him. "Listen," he said, "when old Wish and Matt and Kevin get here, I want you to tell them how that bull got me. Really bloody it up. We'll gross 'em out!"

"Yeah," she said, seeming to mentally hug herself, "we'll gross 'em out!"

Joan stepped into the room. "Gross whom out?"

Only then did it occur to Griff that perhaps he should have checked this thing out with Joan *first.* He stifled a groan and sent her a pleading look. "Uh, this old buddy of mine is coming over later with his two boys."

"Watsons," Danna added flatly.

"Kevin and Matt?" Joan asked, sounding surprised.

"And *Shelley,*" Danna snickered, her hand covering her mouth and nose.

"Shelley? I thought their mother's name was Renae."

Danna giggled. Griff scratched his jaw. "Shelley is...their father's name."

She put one hand on her hip. "I distinctly recall Kevin telling me that his father's name was Wish."

"Nickname," Griff said. "He got it by constantly *wish*ing his name wasn't Shelley."

"Because you and your friends teased him about it, no doubt," she huffed.

He tried to look contrite and apparently failed.

Joan looked down at her daughter. "I'll have you know, young lady, that Shelley can sometimes be a boy's name as well as a girl's name, and you shouldn't make fun of a person just because his name is a little . . . unusual."

Danna stared up at her dolefully, her teeth clamping down on her bottom lip. Joan's forbidding expression softened noticeably. She obviously was no more immune to her daughter's innocent wiles than anyone else. Griff smiled to himself and cleared his throat.

"Ah, why don't you ask her why the Watsons are coming over?" he suggested.

Joan glanced at him, then back at her daughter. "Danna? What's this about?"

Danna stuck out her chin. "I told Kevin that Griff Shaw was staying with us, and he told his brother, and Matt said I was a liar—"

"What?"

Danna nodded emphatically. "'Cause Griff Shaw is a rodeo star, he said, and we don't know any! But we do! So Griff called Shel—Mr. Watson and . . ." She screwed up her face trying to remember the rest. "They couldn't come tomorrow!"

Joan turned to Griff. "You invited them over?"

Of course he had invited them over! "Anybody could have claimed to be me on the telephone," he argued.

"Do you know what you've done?" she snapped, glaring at him.

His mouth was hanging open. "I've proved your daughter is no liar, for one thing!"

"Now everyone will know you're here!"

"So? The whole church knew anyway, didn't they?"

"No!"

"But—"

"I don't want this whole town thinking we're living together!"

"But we are living together," Danna piped up in confusion.

Joan turned a horrified stare down at her and then a blazing one at *him!* "How could you?" she demanded. "Do you want to ruin me?"

"For Pete's sake, this isn't the last century!"

"I'm a teacher! An elementary-school teacher! And this is a relatively small town. And you! Everyone knows what a Romeo you are!"

What could he say to that? Danna had her own question. "What's a romelo?"

Joan leapt as if she'd been scalded, and her look said that this, too, she laid at his door. "Never mind, honey. Your snack is ready. Why don't you go on into the kitchen?"

Danna sighed and dragged her feet toward the door. "Mommy," she said, glancing back over her shoulder, "can't they come? Matt'll say I'm a liar for sure if they can't come."

Joan closed her eyes. "Don't worry, Danna, no one's going to call you a liar. After this, the whole town will know you've got Griff Shaw in this bedroom!"

Danna smiled. "All right!" She fairly skipped out of the room. Joan glared at Griff, then followed her daughter.

Griff put his head back and groaned, but he immediately sat upright again, once more aware of the paper that crackled and whispered in his lap. He turned it and gazed down at the picture, a smile slipping across his face. Why, he wondered, couldn't he work the same magic with the mother that he seemed to work with the daughter? And why did it matter so much? She was just a woman after all.

He shook his head. Some *Romelo.*

He chuckled.

And some kid. Some very special kid.

Chapter Five

Joan listened to the raucous laughter and willed herself not to be bitter or small about it. She reminded herself that the Watsons were there for Danna's sake. Danna was the one Matt had called a liar, the one whose feelings had been hurt, the one whose pride had been wounded. She was just realizing, too, that her daughter would be something of a celebrity among her classmates when she returned to school. Word would definitely be out by then. Matt Watson was awestruck by the famous bull rider, but no more so than his own father. Most shocking of all, though, was the fact that Mrs. Watson had come with them, displaying all the signs of an infatuated rodeo groupie! Joan had left the room the moment the other woman had clasped Griff's hand in both her own and squealed with delight. Joan sighed. She'd be lucky if it wasn't printed on the front page of tomorrow's newspaper that Griff Shaw was here. If the Watsons were so enamored of him, she asked herself cryptically, why didn't they just box him up and take him home with them?

She thumbed through her magazine, as irritated with herself as with the rest of them because she couldn't seem to forget that they were all in there having a good time while she sat here pouting on the couch. Oh, what was wrong with her? She didn't want to be around the man at all. She had come in here of her own accord, so why should she feel left out and . . . lonely?

It struck her suddenly that that was exactly how she was feeling, exactly how she had been feeling for this whole week. But why? She had never been lonely when it had been just her and Danna, not like this anyway. Logically, adding another person to the household should have increased her desire for privacy rather than company, but somehow it wasn't working out that way. Somehow she had gotten isolated in her own private world while Griff and Danna and apparently everyone else enjoyed a special friendship.

Why was it that everyone but her seemed to like the man? The ambulance attendants, Bolton Charles. Why, the two older women who took turns sitting with him every day fairly doted on him! And her daughter. Heaven help them both, Danna was besotted with the man. That, she supposed, was what hurt most. Well, he wouldn't be here forever.

The doctor had told her that Griff could get up on his crutches again next week as long as he didn't overdo it. She figured that maybe a week after that the muscle in the leg would be healed well enough for him to start the physical therapy the doctor had also mentioned. His sprains ought to be healed by then, too, and they could stop worrying about the concussion. That left only the broken clavicle and ribs to keep him down. By the first of the year there would be no excuse whatsoever for him to impose on them any longer. Now all she had to do was get through the Christmas holidays. She still hadn't told Danna that they wouldn't be going to Grandma and Grandpa's house for Christmas. She just kept hoping for someone, anyone, to take him off their hands.

Like an unwelcome but recurring nightmare, she heard him call her name, or what passed for her name with him. "Jo? Hey, Jo! Could you lend a hand?"

She had half a mind to sit right where she was, but someone would only come looking for her if she did. Miffed with all of them, herself included, she slid off the couch and stalked across the room and down the hall, then turned sharply into the already crowded room. They were all gathered around the bed, talking and laughing. The chitchat stopped the instant Griff glanced in her direction.

"Honey, would you find us a working pen?"

She had to bite her tongue to keep from telling him what she thought of being called honey and ordered around like a servant. Instead she settled for a glare and swept out of the room. She walked straight to the built-in desk in the kitchen, yanked open a drawer and grabbed a ballpoint pen. Then she marched back to the bedroom and thrust it at him through a small forest of heads and shoulders.

He had the audacity to wink and say, "Thanks, sugar," knowing full well she'd have liked to slap the words right back into his mouth. He was sitting on the side of the bed, one arm draped around Danna's shoulders, that championship smile in place, and wearing that same plain white T-shirt again and a pair of faded red fleece gym pants that she had dragged out of the attic for him. They were a bit small for him, and she noted that as he sat with his legs over the side of the bed his right leg was noticeably swollen from the knee up, not as badly as it had been, but swollen still.

One of the boys shoved a newspaper clipping at him, and he took his arm from around Danna's shoulder long enough to scribble something on it. The boy made an appropriate sound of pleasure as his brother extended a plain piece of paper. Griff spent a little more time wielding the pen than he had before, and the result was a stylized sketch of a bull's head bearing his signature.

The boy showed his obvious pleasure by flattening the paper against his chest and breathing, "Wow!" Then, noticing that his brother seemed a bit crestfallen, he quickly began to gloat. "I got a bull's head *and* Griff's autograph!"

"So?" the other boy sneered. "I got his autograph on his very own article!"

"Boys." Their mother laid warning hands on their shoulders while shooting apologetic glances at Griff, but just then the one with the sketch stuck his tongue out at the one with the clipping and suddenly a shoving match ensued. One of them bumped Griff's leg, causing him to grimace in pain, and the boys' father clamped a hand down on each neck.

"All right, that's it!" Wish Watson declared. "We're gone. You two've handed out enough grief for one evenin'."

"Aw, Da-a-ad, not yet!" they whined, but Wish shook Griff's hand and bade him farewell.

"Good to see you again, old buddy! You take care now, and when Miss Jo over here turns you loose, you come see us, hear?"

Miss Jo? Well, it beat honey and sugar and Red.

Renae Watson had to gush for a few more minutes about how thrilled she was to meet the "real" Griff Shaw, but then they finally took their leave. Joan walked them out, a smile pasted on her face, and strolled back toward Griff's bedroom, shaking her head about this business of autographs and gushing grown-up women. He was a rodeo rider, for pity's sake, not some movie star or... hero. Drawn into the room despite herself, she eased through the door and stopped.

Her little daughter was tucking the big bad bull rider into bed as if he was one of her dollies, her tiny hands smoothing the covers over the side of the bed as she climbed down to the floor. Her little face shone with affection, adoration even. When he slid his hand around to cup the back of her head, she whispered, "Thanks, Griff."

He stroked that bright hair, his smile soft and tender for this little girl. "Anytime, angel. My pleasure. And if those Watson outlaws give you a hard time again, I'll skin their heads for 'em. Okay?"

She grinned. "Okay."

"And that goes for anybody else who bugs my girl, too."

He tapped her on the end of her nose, and she giggled. *Her daddy should be the one to tell her that,* Joan thought. But her "father" never would, and if not this man, then who? She thought suddenly of her own father, how he would sit quietly in his chair, smoking his pipe and reading his paper while she played on the floor beside him. She thought how his hand would drift down occasionally and pat her head or stroke her hair in a kind of absentminded affection. She had always taken his love for granted. He was her daddy. He loved her. It just stood to reason. But there was no daddy for her daughter, not for her own precious little girl. She had to hear these protective noises from a stranger who had stumbled into their lives by pure chance. It was all so monstrously unfair! Joan stepped forward and laid a coaxing hand on Danna's shoulder.

"Come on, sweetie. Let's give Griff a chance to rest. He looks tired."

"Thanks," he murmured, lifting his gaze to Joan.

She ushered Danna toward the door. "Good night, Griff," Danna whispered.

"Good night, princess," he said. "See you in the morning." Smiling, he closed his eyes. Joan would never know what kept her there, why she lingered that extra moment after Danna had left the room, but it was all too clear why her heart leapt when he whispered, "You, Red, I'll be seeing in my dreams."

It was bad news. She just knew it was bad news. Why else would he still be at the doctor's office? If he was at the doctor's office. But of course he was. Where else would he be? Still, his appointment had been made for noon to accommodate Bolton, who had offered to provide transportation and escort. She glanced at the kitchen clock once more, her cup of tea cooling on the table before her: 3:07. More than three hours. It was bad news. It had to be bad news.

Oh, Lord, let him be all right, she silently prayed. *He's a skunk and a world of trouble, but I don't want anything bad to happen to him.* She thought of the swelling she'd been noticing in his knee and bit her lip.

At the very first sound of the door opening, she bolted up and dashed down the hall. He was struggling through the door on his crutches, his face drawn despite his smile. She noticed several things at once. In a cowboy hat, he looked too handsome to be real, for one. His leg was badly swollen, for another, and all the swelling now seemed to be concentrated in his knee. She saw, too, that Bolton was with him, his arms full of wrapped boxes and packages as if they'd been . . .

"Shopping?" she demanded. "I'm worried sick and *you* are out *shopping?*"

Bolton pushed the door closed with his back, while Griff lifted off his hat, balanced on one leg. "You're home early," he said, his smile fading.

"On the last day before the holidays, school always gets out early," she snapped, "and don't change the subject!"

"I wasn't. I mean, I didn't expect you—"

"Griff!" Danna flew down the stairs and threw herself against him, her arms flinging around his legs.

"Whoa!" He stumbled slightly, one hand dropping to her back.

It was then that Bolton stepped forward. "Uh, ladies, I think we better let Griff sit before he falls down."

Griff sent him a grateful look, dropped his hat on a peg in the wall and patted Danna between the shoulder blades. "Sorry if I worried you, honey," he said. "I thought I'd be back before you."

Danna pulled him toward the living room, her fingers curled into the seam of his jeans leg. "Come sit down!"

Chuckling, he hobbled along with her, but Joan was aware that he had already expended a great deal of energy and was quite literally on his last legs. Scowling, she stepped up to his side and slid her arm around his waist, her hand going to his crutch. He smiled, relinquished the crutch and leaned heavily against her, his arm around her shoulders. She ignored the thrill that swept through her, quelled the impulse to jerk away and propelled him doggedly toward the living room and the armchair, Bolton bringing up the rear. He relinquished the second crutch and sank down into the chair with a sigh. Danna began trying to tug his coat off him. He assisted her wearily while Joan propped his crutches against the wall.

"Where do you want these?" Bolton asked at her elbow, indicating with a nod of his head the packages he held in his arms.

"Just set them on the coffee table," Griff said. "Danna can put them under the tree for me later."

Bolton did as requested, then turned his attention back to Griff. "Want me to help you into bed before I go? You look pretty done in."

"To tell you the truth," Griff said, "I'm too tired to try it just now. You go on. I'll manage. And Bolt..." He extended his hand. "Thanks."

Bolton gave it a hearty shake. "You're welcome. Danna, Joan, if you two think you can handle it from here, I'm gone."

"We'll take care of him!" Danna said, an arm draped protectively over his shoulders.

"Yes, thank you," Joan added. "We can manage. Give my best to Clarice."

"I'll do that," he replied, already leaving.

She turned to accompany him, but he was already at the door and through it before she could do more. She turned back to Griff, her hands at her hips, and suddenly her anger boiled over.

"Just what did you think you were doing?" He sent her a look fraught with weary pleading, but all the worry that had been tormenting her earlier was venting itself in the only acceptable manner she could allow. "Of all the stupid, irresponsible, knuckleheaded—"

"I couldn't let Christmas come without having anything to give my two best girls," he said quietly.

Christmas. Her gaze flew to the packages stacked on the coffee table. Christmas gifts. Of course. But she wasn't willing to let go of that protective shield of anger just yet. "I didn't know you had the money to shop for Christmas," she snapped.

His gaze dropped guiltily. "Ever hear of credit cards?"

"I've heard of them," she returned sharply. "I've just never had one, and I have a hard time believing you do, either."

"Look," he said, sighing, "I'm tired. Could we have this argument later?"

Lines of weariness were etched around his eyes and mouth, and she noticed that he had stretched out his injured leg, his shoulders slumping. She bit back a stinging reply and folded her arms.

"Danna," he said, injecting a note of brightness into his voice, "why don't you show me those packages and I'll tell you which ones are yours."

She clapped her hands together and happily did as asked. The boxes were quickly divided into two piles. Joan couldn't help noticing that hers was as large as Danna's. Neither could she prevent a secret pleasure at the prospect of opening all those lovely boxes on Christmas Eve. The last time a man had bought her a gift of any sort was . . . Well, it didn't warrant remembering. Still, it was foolish of him, especially if he had as little money as she suspected he did. It only stood to reason after all, that he wouldn't be here if he could afford to be someplace where he would be genuinely welcomed. And she had made it obvious—painfully obvious, she feared—that that place was not here. In his own home. She swallowed down that unpalatable thought and interrupted the guessing game that had begun.

"That's enough now, Danna. You put the boxes under the tree while I help Griff into bed. He's tired, and he's in pain, and he'd probably like a cup of hot tea." He made a face. "Coffee, then," she said.

He laid his head back. "All I want is a pillow and an ice pack," he said, "and to get out of these tight jeans."

She took a crutch from the wall and handed it to him. Moving slowly, he got himself up on one leg and fitted the crutch under one arm, reaching out for her with the other. She moved to his side and once more slid her arm around his waist, taking his weight across her shoulders. Carefully they moved together out into the foyer and down the hall to his room, where she eased him onto the side of the bed.

"I think you may be right this time, darlin'," he said wearily. "I think I may have overdone it a bit."

She ignored the endearment as well as the flush of pity in favor of righteous indignation. "Anybody with a teaspoonful of gray matter would have known that. You should've come straight home from the doctor's office. Shopping!"

"I'm not sure it was the shopping that did me in," he revealed. "Will you help me with my boots? I've gotta get out of these jeans."

She bent, grabbed the heel and the toe of one boot and began to tug. "What do you mean," she asked, "it wasn't the shopping?" The boot gave and slid off. "What other nonsense were you up to?" She grasped the other boot and tugged more carefully this time because of his injury.

"Well," he said, "I probably shouldn't have gone upstairs first."

"Upstairs!" She stopped what she was doing to gape at him. "You went *upstairs?*"

He leaned back on his elbows, a glint in his eye. "I had to know what sizes to buy, didn't I?"

She couldn't believe she was hearing this, especially when the full import finally hit her. "You went through our things?"

He shrugged innocently. "I just wanted to be sure I had you sized up right."

"I can't believe you went through my... our things!"

"You ought to be glad. I had you pegged a size too big on the bottom."

Her mouth fell open. "I... h-how... of all the..."

"Oh, now, you don't have anything to be ashamed of," he said lightly, his eyes raking over her. "In fact, I'd say just the opposite." He grinned. "Get that other boot now, will you? This leg is killing me."

Angrily she leaned over and yanked off the boot. He sucked in his breath sharply but made no complaint. Instead he simply started undoing his pants. She whirled around and started for the door.

"Oh, come on, Jo, it's no big deal. Besides, I don't think I can peel off these jeans without your help."

"Tough!" she snapped. "So sleep in them."

"Come on, Jo. I'm hurting here!" he said, halting her just outside his door.

It was true, and she knew it, but it galled her that he had had the nerve to climb those stairs—in his condition—and rifle through her things just so he could go out and... and... exhaust himself... shopping for her. Them. Shopping for them. When, she asked herself reluctantly, had anybody ever done such a thing... for her or for Danna? Blast him. She turned around and walked back into the room. He was waiting, expectantly. He grinned and flipped a corner of the bedspread over his lap but, for once, wisely said nothing.

She approached the bed and grasped the hem of his pant legs. "Lift!" she commanded tersely.

He levered his weight onto his forearms, and she started to pull. The left pant leg gave easily. His right leg, she realized with some alarm, was even more swollen than she'd thought, but soon this pant leg, too, began to shift. Finally she straightened, taking the jeans with her. Griff sighed and fell back onto the bed. His right knee, which hung just below the fringe of the bedspread on his lap, was bloated and red.

"Good grief! What have you done now?"

He sighed and lifted a hand to massage his temples. "I didn't *do* anything. Well, not anything new anyway. I guess the doctor in Vegas just missed it."

"Missed what?"

"Could be a bone chip," he said, "or maybe a torn ligament. Doc says it could take surgery to fix it."

"For heaven's sake!"

"Aw, it'll be all right," he said. "I'll just have to hobble around a little longer than I figured. We'll give it some time and see what happens."

And stay here a little longer than I figured, she thought.

He pushed up onto his elbows again and looked at her, his expression more solemn than any she'd seen so far. "You don't mind, do you, Joan?"

She opened her mouth to tell him just how much she minded, but something stopped her. Maybe it was the guileless look on his face or the pathetic swelling in that knee, or maybe it was just good manners. For whatever reason, she closed her mouth and shook her head. One corner of his mouth hitched up in a lopsided grin.

"You don't dislike me as much as you pretend to," he said, "and that's what really scares you, isn't it?"

For a long moment, she could only stare, wondering how he could possibly know that, but then she realized that he didn't, and her sharp tongue came to her defense. "Don't flatter yourself, cowboy!"

He cocked his head. "Okay," he said thoughtfully, "if it's just a matter of my great conceit, as you say, then why don't you come on over here and prove it?"

She couldn't believe she was hearing this. "That's the most absurd—"

"Is it? I could hardly take advantage of you in my present condition. I mean, one elbow to the ribs… So what's to fear? Except that you might like it?"

She would like it, but she wasn't about to admit that to him, so she lifted her chin and looked down her nose at him. He was every inch the male, sprawled there on the bed in his stocking feet, the bedspread flipped across his lap, his shoulders straining at the fabric of his shirt. Not even the swollen, discolored knee or the ugly gash that snaked up his thigh detracted from his virility. But she would resist that attraction no matter what it took, for to do otherwise would be to destroy herself. Again.

She folded her arms, forced as much ice into her gaze and tone as possible and said, "I don't have to prove anything to you. And just for the record, did it never occur to you that there could be nothing special about being with a man who'd have any willing woman anywhere, anytime, any way?"

To her satisfaction, he looked as if she'd slapped him. "It's not like that," he told her softly.

She lifted an eyebrow in doubt. "Isn't it?"

"No," he said thoughtfully, "it isn't. Not this time."

"Only because this time the woman isn't willing," she said cryptically and swept from the room.

She turned down the hallway and continued on into the kitchen, her arms wrapped around a middle fluttering with butterflies. She leaned against the counter and caught her breath, feeling oddly as if she'd just had a very narrow escape, as if she'd just danced with catastrophe and barely managed to miss getting her toes trampled. No sooner had she regained her composure than Danna pushed into the kitchen through the swinging door to the dining room. By the look on her little face, Joan knew she had a definite purpose.

Sure enough, the child marched right up to her and said, "Mom, is Griff going to Gra'ma and Gra'pa's with us for Christmas?"

"Uh, no, honey. I—I don't think the trip would be good for him, and...Grandma and Grandpa don't have room for all of us."

"Oh." Danna chewed her bottom lip, then suddenly looked up. "Then I don't want to go, either."

"Danna!"

"Well, he don't wanna be here by hisself," she insisted, and to Joan's dismay, her lips began to tremble.

"Oh, honey!" Joan dropped to her knees and put her arms around her daughter. "He won't be alone. One of the church ladies said she'd come stay with him."

"But it wouldn't be no fun without him," Danna said, tears spilling down her cheeks.

Joan closed her eyes. "Danna..."

"I'll be special good, Mommy," her daughter vowed, wiping at her eyes. "I don't even care if Santa Claus don't find me this year! Griff's already bought a bunch of stuff for me, see, so it's all right, honest, Mommy. I don't want to go."

Joan was flabbergasted. They'd *always* celebrated Christmas at her parents' home in Oklahoma City, and because they'd moved around so much, Danna had assumed some time ago that Santa wouldn't know where else to find her. Now, suddenly, because of that charming scoundrel in the other room, her sweet little Danna wanted to break with tradition, even at the expense of her Santa delivery! Joan tried the only argument she could think of.

"Honey, Grandma and Grandpa will be very disappointed if they don't get to see us at Christmas."

"They can come here."

"No, honey, they can't. Aunt Amy's already there."

"But, Mommy, Griff needs us to stay *here!*"

"Danna—"

"Please, Mommy." Danna put her arms around her mother's neck and turned sad, pleading eyes up at her, whispering, "Please, please, oh, please!"

Joan didn't know whether to shake her daughter or hug her, but her general inclination was to do the latter even though it meant capitulation. Sighing, she followed her heart, clasping her child to her. "All right," she said, "I'll call Grandma and explain."

Danna covered her face with kisses. "Oh, thank you, Mommy! Thank you, thank you!"

Joan laughed, her exasperation vanishing in the face of her daughter's affectionate gratitude. "Don't worry about Santa, either," she said. "I'll see to it that he finds you this year if I have to call all the way to the North Pole!"

Danna sighed in relief. "Oh, good! I really do want to get some toys!"

"I know you do," Joan told her, "but you were willing to do without them for Griff's sake, weren't you?"

Danna nodded. Joan frowned. "Honey, you do understand that when Griff's well again, he's going to leave, don't you?"

Danna cocked her head. "He'll ride in the rodeo again."

"Yes, and chances are we won't see him anymore after that."

"We'll see him," the little girl said gently.

"No, Danna, I don't think we will."

"He said."

Joan was surprised. "Did he?"

Danna nodded, but her eyes were looking a little troubled. "Anyhow," she said, "we'll have him for Christmas."

"All right."

Suddenly Danna brightened. "What are we gonna get him?" she asked, excitement lifting her voice to a squeak.

"Get him?" Joan echoed, shifting gears more slowly.

Danna's eyes danced. "Something special!"

"For Christmas, you mean?"

Danna clapped her hands. "I know! Let's get him one of those big red hearts with candy in it!"

A box of candy? Joan shook her head. "But, Danna, that's for Valentine's Day, not for Christmas."

"Teacher says it is," she argued.

"What teacher?"

"Sunday school. She said Christmas is love, and hearts are for love, aren't they?"

"Well, yes..."

"Then I want to get him a heart."

Joan looked at the mulish set of her little chin, feeling helpless and frightened and even a bit betrayed. "I—I don't know if I can find one at this time of year, Danna."

"Uh-huh, you can, at the drugstore."

Joan pushed up to standing height. "Well, all right, I'll try."

Danna threw her arms around her mother's legs and hugged her, whispering, "Oh, thank you, Mommy." Abruptly she stepped back and bounced up and down on her toes. "Oh, I'm so happy! Can I tell Griff? Can I?"

Joan put a hand to her head. "I guess, but don't stay long. He's very tired. And knock first!" she called after the child, who was already running down the hall.

Christmas with Griff Shaw! Joan walked to the table and dropped onto a chair. The abandoned cup of tea had cooled and she pushed it away.

How had he become so central to their lives, so important to her daughter? It wasn't fair. *You do a good thing,* she thought. *Put aside your fears to take in a wounded stranger with a bad reputation, and what do you get? Your daughter wants to send him love tokens and practically make him a member of the family!* And he was going to hurt them, Danna and her. He was going to hurt them, and she couldn't seem to do anything to stop it. No matter how hard she tried, he just kept getting closer and closer.

Worst of all, she feared the moment would come when she would want him to, and then he would have them right where he wanted them. And after that...after that he would go, and she would be left trying to explain to a broken-hearted little girl how they came to be abandoned not by one man, but by two.

It wasn't fair. It just wasn't fair.

Chapter Six

Griff shot a confused look at Joan over the bright head of the child at his knee. She returned his gaze blandly, allowing no hint of apology to show through. He looked down once more at the box within a box on his lap. Gingerly he reached inside and lifted off the heart-shaped lid.

"Candy!" he exclaimed, his enthusiasm sounding only slightly forced. "Just what I wanted."

"It's a heart!" Danna said needlessly. "For love!"

Joan watched as the full import of the gift sank in. She saw the flicker of surprise in his eyes and the glowing warmth that followed. She watched him swallow down the lump in his throat and take a deeper than usual breath as uncertainty settled over him. Then she recognized decision in the squaring of his shoulders and the firming of his jaw. He lifted his gaze to hers and held it for what seemed a very long time before dropping his attention to Danna, but what he would say, Joan couldn't guess.

With one hand he smoothed Danna's hair, while the other cupped her chin. "You are the most beautiful, wonderful little girl in the whole wide world, and I love you very much." He kissed her on the forehead, and she leaned over the arm of the couch to reach toward him. He bent forward so she could wrap her arms around his neck in an exuberant hug.

"You won't go 'way, will you, Griff?" she said into the curve of his neck.

For a long moment, he seemed to freeze, so long that Danna lifted her head to stare up at him. Joan knew the instant he made up his mind, for he sent her another look, a silent challenge, then closed his eyes briefly before setting aside the gift. Pulling the little one into his lap, he settled her on his good leg and lovingly smoothed her bright red, Christmas appliquéd sweatshirt. "I won't always live with you, sweetheart," he said, picking his words carefully. "I haven't really lived anywhere for a very long time, but it seems that's changed now, and though I'll still have to go away sometimes, I won't ever stay away too long, either."

"Promise?" she asked softly.

He smiled. "Promise. No matter where I go—or where you and Mommy go—I'll always find a way to stay in touch, and I'll come and see you just as often as I can. I swear it." Apparently satisfied, she leaned against his chest, her head upon his shoulder. He winced at the pressure on his collarbone and ribs but then laid his chin against the top of her head and simply held her. After several silent moments, during which Joan fought the most intense jealousy she'd ever known, he seemed to suddenly remember his gift. "Hey," he said, shifting Danna forward, "want a piece of candy?"

She nodded her head eagerly and slid off his knee to retrieve the box herself. She laid it in his lap, and together they examined the contents, discussing what was likely to be hidden in which chocolate shape. After much debate, Danna chose a coconut cream, while Griff took a nut-filled confection. They bit and chewed, savoring each sticky morsel with absurd facial expressions and pronounced moans of delight. It was so comical Joan had to smile.

In fact, she pretty much had to hand it to Griff Shaw this time. He knew how to make a little girl happy. She could only pray that he'd meant what he'd said, or he'd prove that he knew how to break a little girl's heart, too. Somehow, though, she couldn't quite believe it of him. That had not been a promise given lightly or designed to confuse the issue, and for that, if nothing else, she was grateful.

She quelled her jumbled emotions and let the pair clown around together for a few minutes longer, then suggested it was time to open the remaining gifts so Danna could bathe and settle down in bed before Santa came and caught her awake. Griff put the top back on the candy and talked Danna into sitting next to him on the couch while Joan divided up the boxes under the tree. There was one without a name on it that she had intended to send to her father but had decided at the last moment to give to Griff instead, telling herself that one gift for him would not be enough when she and Danna had five or six each.

When all the presents were all distributed, they played a little game to see who would go first, answering silly questions of Christmas lore designed by Joan to be answered by even the smallest child. Griff caught on quickly that Danna was to be allowed to win and missed such simple questions as how many reindeer pulled Santa's sleigh and the name of Baby Jesus's mother. In short order, having dazzled them both with her superior intelligence, Danna settled in to happily rip apart the pretty wrapping paper and open packages.

Joan was astounded and Danna thrilled to find that Griff had rigged her out in the latest Western style, right down to the hand-tooled belt and a racy little shirt with cutout shoulders. Her own gifts of much-needed overshoes, a new coat, a fur-trimmed cap and a series of bedtime storybooks paled in comparison to pairs of stiff new jeans, Western boots and blouses and a dark purple cowboy hat with a chain of silver coins around the crown.

At Danna's insistence, Griff opened his remaining present next. It was nothing very remarkable and probably not very useful—a small, silver-plated case for business cards—but he turned it over in his hand as if it were made of delicately spun glass. He opened the hinged lid with a flick of his thumb, closed it, opened it, closed it again. Joan could tell that he was both surprised and pleased. After a moment, he lifted the flap on his shirt pocket and slipped the card case inside. Patting the pocket gently, he thanked her with a small, poignant smile.

"Your turn, Mommy!" Danna said. After scrambling down off the couch, she crossed the room and eagerly took up a position at Joan's feet, where she fished a certain small box from the pile. "Do this one!"

Joan pretended surprise both at the package and its hopelessly jumbled wrapping and the white banana hair clip set with tiny silk daisies she found inside. In the store, she had turned her head when Danna had slipped it into her shopping cart after first inquiring most innocently if she liked it. Later she had pretended not to notice when it was placed on the checkout counter with a number of other small items, and she had winked at the cashier when her ingenuous little daughter had quickly slipped the bemused woman four long-hoarded quarters and a nickel, less than one-third of the purchase price. With the gift in her lap, she hugged her daughter, then let herself be talked into sweeping her hair up in back and attaching the curved barrette. She fluffed her hair, the tiny flowers a froth of white and yellow on the back of her head from which her fiery hair burst in a tumbling, curling fall.

"Do you like it?" she asked no one in particular.

"It's very beautiful!" Danna exclaimed.

Griff, too, seemed to approve. "You look like a bride," he told her, and then the color drained from his face as he realized what he'd said. "Uh, that is . . . very nice."

Joan quickly removed the clip and shook out her hair, mumbling to a protesting Danna that she wanted to "save it for something special." For some reason she felt her cheeks turning pink, and the anger that would have kept embarrassment at bay seemed to have deserted her. To cover, she quickly picked up another package, a medium-size box wrapped in shimmering red and topped with a big, white lace bow, and divested it of its decorations. Inside was a pair of tall Western boots with tops made of the softest white leather and toes inlaid with turquoise. Joan was astounded, and while Danna squealed with pleasure, she turned her gaze on Griff.

"You shouldn't have done this!"

"Why not?"

"You shouldn't have spent this much!" Not on her anyway!

He chuckled. "Hey, I'm Griff Shaw. When I walk into a Western-wear store, they fall all over themselves with discounts and special purchases. One of the perks. Like 'em?"

"Well, yes, but—"

"That's all that counts then. Journey on, woman."

Apprehensively she set aside the boots for discussion later and picked up the next box. Divested of ribbon and paper, it yielded a button-up denim skirt lined with white eyelet and sporting a wide ruffle that ended midcalf. Next came a fringed leather vest studded with white beads and turquoise stones, followed by a white blouse with enormous sleeves gathered into six-inch-wide cuffs. All together, the outfit was one she might have chosen for herself—had she ever been able to afford such finery. It was also far too much to accept from this man, but Danna was so appreciative and Griff seemed so enormously pleased with himself that Joan found she could make only the most token protest.

"You should have saved your money to pay your doctor bills," she said.

He looked a little guilty at that, but then assured her that he would get the medical bills paid. He was not the sort, he told her, to leave funds owing overlong. "And I don't want to hear any more about it."

She swallowed any further complaint, admitting only in the deepest recesses of her heart how thrilled she was with his selections. When Danna pointed out that the banana clip would look good with her new outfit, she laughingly replied, "Well, so it will," and hugged to herself the secret vision of what she would look like wearing Griff's and her daughter's gifts combined.

A glance at the clock told her that it was past time for Danna to be in bed. Setting aside her own gifts, she helped Danna gather up hers, then watched as the child kissed Griff good-night before hustling her upstairs and into her pajamas. They enjoyed a bedtime story together from one of the new books, then got on their knees for evening prayers. Danna had a great deal for which to be thankful that Christmas Eve, and at the top of her list, right after Mommy and before Grandma or Grandpa, Aunt Amy, her best friend, Samantha, or her delightful gifts, came Griff Shaw. At last, Danna crawled beneath the covers and allowed her mother to tuck her in. Sleep still seemed a long way away for an excited little girl, but Joan knew that she would snuggle down and do her best to dream, never daring to creep from her bed or peek out her door, lest Santa's elves catch her.

Joan mused that it had been a most unusual holiday thus far as she descended the stairs. She let herself into the garage through the end of the hall, passing Griff's bedroom door on the way. The light was on and the door was closed, so she assumed that he was turning in for the night. He wouldn't need her help as he wasn't wearing boots or those tight jeans, having chosen instead an old pair of tennis shoes and jeans so faded and worn that they couldn't have been stiffened much even with starch. "Leftovers from early days," he called them. In the garage, she removed Danna's Santa gifts from beneath the old quilt she had used to hide them and carried them into the house. She piled them in the middle of the floor, then went into the kitchen to remove the stocking stuffers from a top shelf in the cabinet. When she returned, it was to find Griff sitting on the edge of the couch, holding a doll's tiny garment in his hand, his crutch propped next to him.

He shook his head at the scrap of lace fashioned into a gown and accessorized with a tiny tiara, a minuscule scepter and "ruby" slippers. "What will they think of next?" he asked.

"I don't know. Seems pretty sophisticated for a five-year-old, doesn't it?"

"Yeah, but it fits." He shifted his gaze up to meet hers. "She's a real little princess, you know."

Joan nodded. "I think so."

He laid down the plastic encased doll's outfit and picked up a box containing a china tea set. "What I want to know," he said distractedly, "is what kind of an idiot abandons a kid like her?"

Joan blinked at the sudden turn in the conversation. "What?"

He shrugged and traded the tea set for a pink-and-white teddy bear. "I understand the breakup of a marriage," he went on. "Adults do things to one another, disappoint one another, betray one another, but a kid? A baby? How do you cut that out of your life? Lord, she isn't even my kid, and I can't just walk away and pretend she never happened. How can he?"

Was this Griff Shaw talking, a patented member of Dan's Use 'Em and Lose 'Em Club? Obviously she had misjudged him on one or two points. She gave him a look that blatantly said so. "Why, Griff, I do believe you're showing signs of humanity after all."

He actually seemed shocked. "Is that how you see me, like *him?*"

"Well... not entirely," she murmured.

He ran a hand over the back of his neck in agitation. "Answer a question, all right? How'd he get to you?"

She targeted her gaze on the small sack of goodies in her hands. "I thought he loved me," she said quietly. "He lavished a great deal of attention on me. He was terribly charming, very romantic, but it was like a big game to him. He told me later that it was just that I was the only girl he couldn't get into bed. I was holding out for marriage, so he married me. But he never intended to be faithful. He never intended to stay. He played around right from the start, and as soon as this wealthy older woman came along, he dumped me for her."

Griff swore under his breath. Finally he said, "I'm not like that. I wouldn't lie to you, make promises I never intended to keep, not to you or any woman. That's not my style."

She had to smile and shake her head. "Just fun and games, is that it, Griff?"

"Something like that," he muttered.

"No woman's ever had a hold on you, has she?"

"I wouldn't say that," he replied uncomfortably. "It just never worked into anything serious. I thought it might a time or two, but... things just didn't work out."

She nodded. "Okay, so you're not a carbon copy of my ex. Feel better?"

He practically glowered at her. "I don't know how I feel."

She had to laugh. She just had to. He sounded so put upon, so... abused. She, on the other hand, felt oddly reassured, not that she was ready to let her guard down by any means. Still, she was beginning to think that maybe she had overreacted somewhat to his initial "overtures." He wasn't a rapist after all, just an extremely attractive man whose values happened to differ from hers, which was reason enough to resist deeper involvement with him. But that didn't mean friendship was out of the question, did it, especially in view of his relationship with her daughter? She pointed to a large, flat box on the bottom of the pile. "That contains all the pieces of a small table and matching chairs. Why don't you make yourself useful and put them together? It's not supposed to require any tools, but I have a few things if you need them."

He pulled the box out from under the pile and turned it over to take a look at the illustration. "I think I can handle it."

"Good."

They worked separately in silence for some time. Joan opened packages and prepared to set up the tea party she envisioned for her daughter's Santa surprise, while Griff screwed legs on tables and tapped spindles into holes to assemble the chairs. Less than forty minutes later, the setting was complete. The small, maple-finish table and chairs stood before the lit Christmas tree. A dainty, hand embroidered cloth covered the table, the teapot and matching sugar and creamer in its center. Two places were set with saucers, cups, spoons and real linen napkins. A number of small, colorful cookies were arranged on a serving plate and a single tiny rosebud stood in a finger-size china vase. The teddy bear occupied one chair, his arm held out as if in invitation.

Arranged beneath the tree was a wardrobe of doll clothes, several of them made by Joan herself, and a clever wooden case in which to contain them. There were cheap coloring books, as well, and a new box of crayons. For Danna's stocking, Joan had purchased a juicy orange, a crisp apple, a perfect yellow banana and a variety of nuts still in the shell, as well as a large peppermint stick and a small bouquet of suckers.

Griff had moved to the floor in front of the coffee table to give himself room to maneuver without hurting himself, and he stayed there, his bad leg stretched out before him. When she had arranged the display to please her, she cleared away the debris of unnecessary packaging. He scooted across the floor to switch on the television and catch the tail end of the late news. With the sound turned down low, there was nothing to disturb Danna, so Joan didn't mind. When she returned from the kitchen, bearing a second plate of cookies and a glass of milk for Santa to sample, the opening credits of an old movie were rolling across the screen.

"Have you seen this?" he asked, a kind of eagerness lighting his eyes.

"Been a long time," she replied, amused by his interest.

"Let's watch it. Want to?"

"Might as well."

"Turn off the lamp and toss me a pillow from the couch, will you?"

"All right." She did as asked and secured a pillow for herself, as well.

He put his behind him and leaned against the side of the coffee table. She looked around, considering the best angle from which to view the set, and decided that Griff had the best idea. Her usual spot in the armchair would yield her nothing but a good view of the side, back and top of his head, but he looked so comfortable that she didn't have the heart to ask him to move to the couch. She plopped her pillow down next to him, not too close, and sat cross-legged on top of it. With the sound so low, it was necessary to listen carefully, so no one spoke until the two stars swept into a clever dance number, at which point Griff chuckled and said, "I love this."

Joan marveled at his enthusiasm for and enjoyment of this rather corny, highly romanticized old movie. The macho bull rider was the last man she would have expected to indulge in this type of sentimentality. Then again, she hadn't expected the kind of commitment he had made earlier to her daughter, either. She cautioned herself that only time would tell if he meant to or could honor his promise to Danna, and yet her opinion of Griff Shaw was undergoing changes she couldn't seem to prevent.

A commercial came on touting a certain pickup truck, and Griff actually asked what she thought about the product. "I haven't owned a vehicle in years," he said. "I've been flying around this country so long, making do with rental cars and cabs, that I don't even know for sure what's out there, but I kind of like the looks of this thing."

Joan agreed that it was an attractive vehicle, but its popularity, in her opinion, had made it overpriced.

"Hmm, you could be right," he said, rubbing his chin. "What would you suggest?"

She had heard that another American-made model was a good buy and an excellent vehicle, but she admitted that she had had no personal experience whatever from which to draw. Still, to her surprise, he seemed to value her opinion, and she found that she not only enjoyed his company but enjoyed the movie more for it. She offered him the cookies and milk meant for Santa. He declined the milk.

"I'm not much on cow juice," he said. "We lived on a ranch when I was small, you know, used to keep a few milkers, got ours fresh from the cow. I can't get used to this pasteurized, watered-down stuff, especially if its cold. Besides, the way I see it, cow milk is meant for baby cows."

"Oh, great! Don't pass that bit of wisdom on to my daughter, if you please."

He chuckled, scooping up cookies. "Wouldn't think of it, as the slight possibility exists that it's good for her."

She put her head back and laughed. "All right. You get the cookies, I get the milk, and Danna gets the fairy tale."

He swallowed the cookie he was chewing and sent her a measuring look. "You really go out of your way to see that she has everything a kid could want, don't you?"

She shrugged. "She's my daughter, the best thing that ever happened to me. Naturally I give her everything I can. I want her to enjoy her childhood as I enjoyed mine, but it's tough sometimes, being a single parent. Teaching is a demanding job, and it doesn't pay very well for the first several years. We've really struggled."

"That's how you came to be here, isn't it?" he asked.

She nodded. "The rental market is pretty tight around here, and I just couldn't afford a real house for us, so we were living in this tiny efficiency apartment. We don't have much, so space wasn't the real problem, but there was no privacy, and she was the only kid in the whole apartment block. It just wasn't a good setup, so when this deal came along, it was too good to pass on."

"The preacher said he recommended you to Frankie."

"Mmm-hmm, he did, and her to me."

Griff grinned, shaking his head. "She's something, isn't she?"

"Oh, yes. I can't believe she's seventy-six. She seems younger somehow, spunkier."

"She's always said I kept her young," he mused. "I have to wonder about that, though. I haven't exactly lavished her with attention these past few years. I guess I just assumed she'd always be here. This whole thing, her being in Florida and me not even knowing it, the broken hip and all, it's got me thinking. She can't live forever, and when the time comes... Well, I don't want to be looking back and wishing I'd spent more time with her."

"I'm glad to hear that," she told him softly.

His smile was warming. "I'm glad she has friends like you. I don't know what either one of us would have done without you."

"She's done me more favors than I've done her," Joan said dismissively. "In case you don't know, we only pay utilities here."

"Preacher told me."

"That preacher seems to tell you a lot," she muttered.

"He's all right," Griff said. "To hear Frank tell it, he's darn near perfect, so I sort of expected a goody-goody, you know? But he's not like that. He's a regular Joe."

Joan suppressed a giggle. "You call your grandmother, *Frank?*"

He waggled his head side to side ambivalently. "It's an old habit."

She sensed there was more to the story. "Oh?" He popped another cookie into his mouth, chewed it and swallowed, but she wasn't about to let him off the hook that easily. "You were saying?"

He grimaced. "Look, it's no big deal. It's just...you know how boys can be."

"No, actually I don't."

He rubbed his hands on his thighs. "Let's just say that a kid who actually prefers his grandmother's company to that of his friends is apt to take some serious ribbing about it. So, whenever one of the guys suggested some outing but I'd already made plans with her... It was just easier to say I was busy with 'Frank' and leave it at that."

"They, of course, thought Frank was a guy," she pressed, amused when he nodded reluctantly.

"Hey," he said defensively, "they had moms and dads to take for granted. They couldn't have understood how important she was to me even if I could have explained it to them, which I couldn't."

"I see."

Compassion swept through her, compassion for the little boy who had lost both parents when the tractor-trailer rig they were driving in had been hit by a train. Frankie had told her all about it, but she was only now beginning to understand how traumatic it must have been for him. Maybe that was why he wanted to be there for Danna, why he was drawn to her. They shared the loss of a parent in common. She began to believe that he would keep his word to her little daughter. She finished the milk and set the glass on the coffee table next to the half-empty plate of cookies. Danna would naturally assume that Santa had taken his fill and left the rest behind.

They turned their attention back to the movie, and for perhaps the first time since she'd found him passed out on this very floor, Joan actually relaxed in Griff's presence, so much so that she hardly noticed when he stretched his arm out along the top of the coffee table. Only later, when his hand lightly brushed her upper arm, did she realize that he had edged closer and was sitting with his arm practically around her!

She shifted away from him, only to bring more pressure on her arm from his hand. A glance to the side told her that he was focusing on the movie, and she found that she was strangely reluctant to make an issue of that arm. She *wanted* to trust him. She told herself that she wanted to trust him for Danna's sake, but even then, in some small part of her mind, she knew that she was attracted to this man as she never had been to another. She stretched her legs out in front of her and tried to recapture her relaxed mood.

Later, when he tightened his hold and then turned his head to look at her, she knew she had made a big mistake, but then his gaze dropped suddenly to her mouth, and she couldn't move or catch her breath in order to speak. But what did it matter? she thought. It was just a kiss, a simple, harmless... But the emotions that swamped her the instant his mouth covered hers were anything but simple, and all of them were heightened by the fact that the fit was so achingly perfect.

What surprised her most was the softness of his lips, the gentleness of his kiss as his mouth parted over hers, enticing her to do likewise. She responded mechanically, her will seeming to trail well behind her thoughts, which were jumbled at best. He deepened the kiss, turning toward her and bringing his other arm around her. She meant to put her hands against his chest, but they wound up on his shoulders, no impediment at all when he pulled her tightly against him. She felt his heartbeat quicken, felt it thudding against her breast. Then his hands were in her hair, tilting her head to afford him greater access, and his tongue slid into her mouth, hot and wet and silky.

She heard the moan but didn't recognize it as hers. She felt his sleek hair between her fingers but did not realize that she had moved her hands to the back of his head. She felt strength in the arms around her, obscuring her own weakness. But it was all overshadowed by something else, something she had never expected to feel again—desire.

It swept through her with cruel abandon, enlivening her body, sensitizing her every nerve ending, so that when his hands began to roam over her, she could only respond with tiny jerks and gasps and much trembling. She knew the moment his hand dropped to her waist what was coming next, but even then she couldn't seem to react in a way that would stop it. She held her breath as he moved his hand up her rib cage. Then he lifted it and covered her breast and she cried out, her head falling back and breaking the kiss, freeing his mouth to journey along the curve of her throat, scorching her every place it touched.

"Oh, no," she said, "please don't," but she couldn't have moved away at that moment if her very life had depended on it.

He moved his mouth to her ear, whispering, "Shh, it's all right." His hand tightened on her breast, sending shock waves through her, as his mouth skimmed across her face to find hers once more. His kiss was fierce this time, possessive, demanding.

A dozen different scenes flashed through her mind, dream sequences of which she had only been dimly aware, secret desires she had not, did not, want to face. How could this be happening? How could she want this man, this dangerous man, so deeply? She had not felt so alive, so female in a very long time, too long. It was glorious, and she didn't want to give it up, even knowing that she was playing with fire, even with her every protective instinct telling her that she was going to be hurt.

Oh, if only it was real... If only it was love rather than mere desire. But no, Griff Shaw was not the sort of man to love a woman like her. He would never let anything have that much sway over him. His life-style was not conducive to strong personal attachment or fidelity, but she was having difficulty concentrating on that fact with his mouth moving so expertly over hers, his hands so sure upon her body.

He shifted his weight and lay back, pulling her down on top of him. A simple roll reversed their positions. To take his much greater weight off her, he shifted to the side and pushed up onto one elbow, his mouth plying hers skillfully. His hand slipped beneath her sweater and skimmed her bare flesh, sending any thought of resistance spinning off into space. When his fingers closed once more over her breast, she knew she was lost, and she didn't care. Somehow she just didn't care.

It was inevitable. Hadn't she known from the beginning that this was possible? Hadn't she sensed that he could do this to her? It was this—her reaction to this devastating man—that lay at the bottom of her fear. It was this she had hoped to avoid, this she had rightly fought against, what he could make her feel, what he could make her want, that he could make her stop caring about the danger. Somehow, in some part of her, she had known that this could, would, happen, and she was tired of fighting it. She was tired of being alone, and just admitting that to herself brought a sense of relief so profound that she felt tears fill her eyes and leak from beneath her closed lids, and it was then that he withdrew, then that he suddenly wrenched his mouth from hers and lurched away. He had scrambled up onto one knee and then into a sitting position on the coffee table before she fully realized that he had abandoned her.

"Griff?"

He groaned and dropped his head into his hands. "Get out of here, Jo."

She sat up, confused. "I don't understand. What's wrong?"

He laughed harshly. "What's wrong?" He glared at her. "You're lying there crying while I make love to you, and you want to know what's wrong?"

She could only blink at him. "It—it's not what you think."

He closed his eyes. "Just get out here. Just go to bed. Go up the stairs and to your room. *Now.*"

"But—"

"For pity's sake, Jo!" he shouted. "Don't you get it? I don't want it, not like this!"

He didn't want it. Her. He didn't want her. She covered her mouth with one hand, and with the other she pushed herself up to her feet and bolted from the room. She heard him swearing as she pounded up the stairs, but she couldn't think beyond the pain that enveloped her. She didn't even feel the fresh tears until she was safely closed away behind the door to her room, and even then all she could do was let them fall.

Chapter Seven

"May I speak to you for a minute, Miss Burton?"

"Certainly." Joan looked up from her desk and smiled, but the smile was forced, and the recipient knew it. She looked away again, targeting the paper she was grading, and asked, "Is something wrong, Mr. Miller?"

He walked into the classroom and, to her surprise, closed the door before approaching the desk. "You tell me, Joan. *Is* something wrong? You haven't been yourself since the holidays."

Joan sighed. "I'm sorry, Adam. Have there been any complaints?"

"No. Just concern. You're well liked here, Joan, and your friends are worried about this malaise you seem to have fallen into. You never laugh anymore or really even smile, and there have been certain . . . rumors."

Her head came up at that, a chill sweeping over her. "Rumors?"

He nodded and took up a position on the corner of her desk, one leg swinging gently. He picked up a small crystal paperweight in the shape of an apple and turned it over in his hand. Joan had admired his hands before. They were smoothly knuckled and well manicured, large, as a man's hand should be, with long, blunt fingers. They were able hands, like Adam Miller himself. He prided himself, she knew, on a tightly run organization—and his grooming. He had the demeanor and look more of a bank president than an elementary-school principal.

Nevertheless, he was a fair and authoritative administrator, to whose name no major scandal had ever been attached, despite, or so she had heard, a rather nasty divorce several years ago and a long, public relationship, now defunct, apparently, with a teacher at the high school. He was, she judged, somewhere in his mid forties. His silver blond hair was thinning slightly at the crown, but his eyes remained a startling green, and the cleft in his jutting chin added definition to an otherwise mundane face with even but blunt features. He was well liked and friendly despite a professional aloofness that clearly proclaimed his superior position to the many women who worked in the building. It was that unapologetic aura of superiority that now told Joan his concern was professional as well as personal. She sat back in her chair and waited, her attention all his.

Adam put down the paperweight and straightened the line of his charcoal gray suit coat before smoothing his silk tie. Composed, he broached the subject. "We all know that you moved into the Thom house around Thanksgiving," he began. "At the time, it was said to be a kind of house-sitting arrangement."

"Something like that," she confirmed.

He nodded and adjusted the knot of his tie. "And now," he said, "it's rumored that the great rodeo legend himself is in residence."

Joan closed her eyes briefly and determined what she would say. "Ah, yes, that's true. What may not be common knowledge, however, is the fact that he's recovering from... some very serious wounds."

The principal nodded consideringly. "Actually, I had heard that he was gored. In Las Vegas, wasn't it?"

"I believe so."

"Um, one wonders how he came to be in Duncan if his wounds were so serious. Las Vegas isn't exactly next door."

"Oh, two friends flew with him to Oklahoma City and drove him down here. This is his home after all, and... well, rodeo performers seem to have a rather difficult time acquiring hospitalization insurance."

"I see."

Joan rushed on, hoping to elicit his full understanding. "His grandmother is in Florida, visiting a friend for the winter, but she would have come home to... tend him herself if she hadn't suffered an accident of her own." She waved a hand dismissively. "Something about a duck. Anyway, she's mending a broken hip now, so... my minister arranged to have some ladies from my church come in during the day." She added that last bit to let him know that she had nothing to hide. Still, she didn't like the way he was looking at her, as if he was measuring everything about her.

He slid a hand into his pants pocket and jingled his change, saying, "And has Mr. Shaw been... an amenable patient?"

How to answer that one? She cocked her head. "Well, he's... had his moments."

"Ah. And are you... content to have him there?"

She took a deep breath. "I wouldn't say that exactly."

He folded his hands together. "All right. Let's approach this another way, shall we? Has he made a pass at you?"

Her mouth fell open and hot, bright color rose to her cheeks. *Made a pass?* she thought wildly. *He passed, all right.* Fresh humiliation swamped her, and she turned her face away.

Adam Miller cleared his throat. "Never mind," he said. "You don't have to answer that. I know what I need to in order to determine my own course of action."

His course of action? She snatched a paper from the desk and fanned herself. "I—I don't understand."

He got to his feet, carefully adjusting his clothing, giving special attention to the lie of his jacket across his shoulders and the evenness of his cuffs. "I'm very protective of my teachers, Joan, and my friends. I think perhaps I should speak to Mr. Shaw, judge his condition for myself. I wouldn't want him to...take advantage of your generosity." He reached out and curled a finger beneath her chin. "I'd like to put the smile back on that pretty face," he said before abruptly taking back his hand and smoothing down the front of his coat. "Why don't we say dinner?" he went on briskly, taking advantage of her speechlessness. "That should give me enough time to determine his condition, not to mention his intentions, and find the best way to put him in his place. Would seven be appropriate?"

"Seven?" she echoed.

His smile was almost piteous. "For dinner. If that's too late for your little girl, you could always feed her earlier."

Her eyes widened as she thought of Danna, Griff Shaw and Adam Miller at the same table. She choked down a tendency toward wild, hysterical laughter and murmured in a strangled voice, "Yes, that would definitely be best."

"Fine," he said, sounding very pleased as he dropped a heavy hand onto her shoulder. "Don't worry about dessert. I'll bring it with me. Well, I'll see you at seven then."

She shot him an exasperated look and briefly considered telling him that tonight would not be convenient and, furthermore, that he had no right to invade her home, but there was the possibility that this might be the nudge Griff needed to at last be on his way. It had been nearly a month after all, and despite what she'd said to Adam, the church ladies were no longer coming in during the day to baby him. He seemed to be making do quite nicely, even with the monstrous brace he was now wearing on his knee. She closed her eyes, envisioned having her home and her daughter to herself, and let Adam Miller walk out without making the slightest protest. Was it cowardly, she wondered, to let him do her dirty work? But then she thought realistically of the evening ahead and knew that it was going to be, at best, an ordeal, but so be it. She wanted her life back, all of it—her home, her child, her thoughts, her dreams, her emotions—and every day shared with Griff Shaw brought her dangerously closer to losing even her pride.

What was it with him? she wondered. Why, after Christmas Eve, did he continue to flirt and tease and pretend an interest she knew he didn't truly feel? It was as if he sought constantly to remind her that she was the one who had almost yielded to desire. She had recently asked him, demanded to know, actually, what he wanted from her, and he had merely looked uncomfortable and murmured that he didn't know himself. The situation was intolerable. She found herself close to tears several times a day. She dreaded going home and seeing him, yet could not seem to sidetrack her steps when they carried her to his room.

He had been coming to the table for dinner in the evening since he'd gotten the knee brace and had even provided it a few times, once phoning for pizza and another time concocting a hideous brown glop he'd called chili. Danna had liked it, or so she'd claimed, but Joan's stomach had rebelled at the very sight of it, and she'd contented herself with a serving of the green salad he'd put together. Other times, he'd warmed up accumulated leftovers or merely shared the bounty brought in by one of the church ladies until their visits dwindled to a stop. If he could do *that,* Joan reasoned, he could manage on his own. Maybe he couldn't ride the rodeo circuit again, but he could finish his recuperation elsewhere, couldn't he ? Even if it was his house.

She didn't want to think about that or anything else, except getting rid of Griff Shaw. She'd worry about living arrangements—and Adam Miller—later. She quickly finished grading papers, then turned her mind to dinner. She could do something simple like spaghetti, but for some reason that didn't appeal. Lasagna maybe. But no, that didn't sound much better. She wanted something festive, something *different.* She chewed her lip until inspiration struck. Pineapple-glazed chicken. Brown rice. But the rice would take a long time to cook. She had to get moving. Swiftly she made a shopping list, then gathered her things together and left.

The fact that Danna was now going straight home on the bus after school saved her some precious time. Danna was going to be heartbroken when Griff left, but she would get over it, especially if he managed to see her from time to time. But not too often. She didn't think she could stand it if he was there every time she turned around. Well, they'd just have to work something out. She and Danna had been happy before Griff Shaw, they'd be happy after him. Period.

She made a quick stop by the grocery before heading north on 81 and turning back west on Plato Road until she reached the neighborhood where Griff had built his house. Funny, she had started out thinking of it as Frankie's house, and somehow now she couldn't think of it belonging to anyone ultimately but Griff Shaw. She knew that his name was on the title, that Frankie had insisted on that. And yet it was home. Somehow it was home for her and Danna.

She pulled into the driveway, parking not in her usual place by the front door but beyond it, near the garage, which she had never gotten in the habit of using. Griff had said something about a garage door opener, but she hadn't paid much attention. Maybe he would have one installed for Frankie after she got home, but Joan didn't want to think about that, either. She gathered up the groceries and headed to the door. She was juggling sacks and trying to get a hand on the knob when the door suddenly opened.

"Mommy! Guess what?"

"What, honey?"

"It's a surprise!"

"A surprise?" Joan groaned. "Griff isn't making dinner, is he?"

"No! It's a baby!"

"What?"

Griff came flying into the foyer on his crutches, laughing. "The Charleses," he said. "Bolt and Clarice have a new baby girl. He called a few minutes ago."

"A girl!" Joan said. "I thought they were expecting another boy."

"Well, they were," he confirmed. "That's why it's such a surprise."

"Isn't it too early?" she worried.

"It's early, but baby and mother are fine. Apparently they were concerned about the toxemia, so they induced her this morning. Anyway, the preacher's walking on air. They've named her Melanie, Melanie Helene Charles. Isn't that sweet?"

"Sweet," Joan murmured, amazed at his enthusiasm.

"Here," he said, "let me help." He put aside one of the crutches, pulled a grocery bag into the curve of his arm and hobbled toward the kitchen.

Joan shrugged out of her coat and hung it and her scarf on a peg on the wall. She'd return and put it away later. When she got to the kitchen, Griff was unloading the groceries onto the table.

"Chicken for dinner?" he asked. "Sounds good. I'm starved."

"Well, you may want to have a snack, then. Dinner won't be ready until seven."

"Oh? How come?"

She opened the refrigerator door and started rearranging things. "We're having company," she muttered.

"What?"

"I said, we're having company," she snapped, whirling around.

He just looked at her and shrugged. "Okay, that's cool. So who is it?"

For some reason, his reasonable attitude irritated her. She started shoving groceries into the refrigerator. "Adam Miller."

"Who?"

She slammed the refrigerator door. "Adam Miller!"

"And who," he asked, "is Adam Miller?"

She glared at him to let him know that she resented the question, then said, "The principal at my school."

He gawked. "Your boss?"

She folded her arms. "What of it?"

"Holy cow!" he said. "The living room's a wreck!"

"Oh, no!"

"We were playing tea party," he explained hastily. "Uh, I'll take care of it. You start dinner, and I'll pick up in the other room, then..." He looked down at the T-shirt he was wearing. "I'll change. I—I'll even see to it that Danna is presentable. Oh, and I probably ought to take a look at the powder room, huh?"

"Don't worry about Danna," she said lightly.

"Aw, it's no trouble."

Joan turned away, saying carefully, "Danna won't be joining us for dinner." She sensed that he had gone very still.

After some time, he said simply, "Oh?"

Joan plucked up her courage and turned around, lifting her chin. "I don't see why she should have to wait until Adam can get here. She's used to an early dinner after all."

Griff narrowed his eyes. "Adam," he said, nodding as if he'd reached some sort of conclusion. "An elementary-school principal, who doesn't like kids."

She had never even thought it, but she knew in that instant that Griff was absolutely right, and it infuriated her. "How dare you say that?" she demanded, barely cognizant of the words tumbling out of her mouth. "You don't even know him, and you're judging him! I'll have you know, he's a wonderful principal and...and a wonderful man."

"And single, I'll bet," Griff surmised dryly.

She threw up her hands. "What of it?"

He didn't answer her, just drilled her with an indefinable look, then turned and hobbled out of the room. She put her hands on the countertop and pulled deep, calming breaths, her head bowed, until she felt calm again. How did he always manage to do this to her? she wondered. He got to her so easily, and it frightened her. It frightened her, too, that he had pegged Adam so neatly. She fought down a surge of uncertainty about the coming evening and doggedly began to prepare dinner.

Griff wet his comb and smoothed his hair back over his ears. He needed a haircut. He needed a tranquilizer. He needed a set of brass knuckles. *Adam,* he thought disgustedly. Something told him that *Adam* was good-looking, tall and very sure of himself. Well, Adam was not going to be staking any claims tonight, or any other night, if Griff could help it. But could he? Griff looked at himself in the mirror.

"Why don't you just tell her?" he asked himself, but he already knew the answer. He was scared, scared to death, and who could blame him? He had never been in love before. He didn't know what the hell he was doing, and she had absolutely no reason to believe him even if he did find the courage to spill his guts. How could she? He found himself, not for the first time, wishing he could break Dan Burton's jaw, but he knew, deep down, that Dan wasn't the only one to blame. He hadn't exactly lived the life of a monk himself, but then he hadn't understood how his lack of self-control could affect his future, destroy his credibility, prejudice a good woman against him. What had she ever done, after all, to be hurt as she had? How was she supposed to trust a man like him? Okay, maybe she was attracted to him, but that only made it worse, in a way.

He leaned his forehead against the mirror and closed his eyes. What was he supposed to do? How did he handle this? He knew how to seduce a woman, but how did he make one love him, really love him? Was there some secret to it, some formula? He sighed and pushed himself away from the sink. Well, he could handle Adam at least. One thing he was very good at was sizing up the competition.

That thought in mind, he walked into the other room, chose a bolo tie from the dresser and slipped it over his head. He worked the black leather cord beneath the collar of his shirt and slid the lapis lazuli catch into place. It was an impressive piece of jewelry and an expensive one considering the size of the stone and the heavy gold setting. He fixed the matching solid gold tips to the points of his black shirt collar, then tucked gold links into his cuffs and buckled the heavy gold chains around the heels and insteps of his black boots. He had forgone his usual jeans for a pair of tightly fitting black Western-style slacks, over which he next put on his knee brace. He wished that he could leave it off for once, but he didn't dare. All that stood between him and the street was that nasty-looking brace. The support in place, he shrugged into his coat, a butter-soft, buff-colored suede jacket in a Western cut, and took a last look. It was definitely the best he could do, given the need for a haircut and the knee brace. All in all, he figured he could give the principal a run for his money.

He was of the same opinion ten minutes later when Joan escorted the interloper into the living room and then departed to put dessert into the refrigerator. Griff set aside the newspaper he was pretending to read and got to his feet, extending his hand. Adam Miller put his own into it and gave a shake. Griff smiled to himself. The man's hand was as soft as a baby's bottom. The nails, Griff noticed derisively, were professionally manicured. Nothing to fear here. He gestured for the other man to take a seat, feeling very much the host. Griff had been sure to seat himself on the couch, knowing that the other man wouldn't want to sit next to him. Sure enough, Adam took the chair, leaving the space on the sofa next to Griff for Joan.

When she returned, lavishing praise on the fruit pie Adam had brought with him, she perched on the edge of the cushion and leaned forward uncomfortably. She had changed her work clothes for a pair of soft melon-colored slacks and a cream white sweater with a cowl neck. She looked great, as usual, and Griff had made certain to tell her so, while leaving Adam no opportunity to follow suit by instantly engaging the man in conversation.

They chatted about the weather, automobiles, mutual acquaintances. Griff made sure that Adam knew one of the local school-board members was an old friend of his. He received with glee the news that Adam's ex-wife was also an old girlfriend. Despite the man's discomfort, Griff was determined to catch up on news concerning his old flame. It seemed that she had remarried and immediately started filling her nursery. The implications were obvious, and Griff could see that they had not escaped Joan. He was actually having a good time.

"Speaking of babies," he said, "some good friends of ours just added a daughter to their family today."

Joan winced when he said "ours," but quickly put on a smile. "Yes," she said, "my minister's wife, Clarice Charles, gave birth to a little girl this afternoon. I'm so happy for them."

"Oh, yeah," Griff said, settling his arm along the back of the couch. "Little girls are so sweet. I can't imagine any man not being thrilled to have a daughter. I mean, what could be better than that?"

Adam looked as if he'd been poked with a needle. "I, um, suppose you might get an argument from the parents of boys," he murmured.

"Ah, well, a son would be okay, too," Griff said, "but I, for one, wouldn't want to miss the experience of a daughter. Danna's taught me that. Have you met her? She's a wonderful little girl, a real angel."

Adam straightened his tie, pretending distraction. "Yes, certainly. She's, ah, been to the school from time to time with her mother. A very well-behaved child, I believe."

"Oh, sure. Absolutely," Griff said. "She's very sensitive, too. She knows when she's not wanted." He said it bluntly, his gaze fixed on Adam Miller. Adam turned red, partly from embarrassment, partly, Griff knew, from guilt. Joan knew it, too. The fact that she wouldn't look at either one of them proved it, as far as Griff was concerned. He decided he'd made his point and smoothly changed the subject. He laid a proprietary hand on Joan's shoulder and said, "Hon, maybe Adam would like a cup of coffee or a glass of tea."

She sent him a scathing glare, but then turned a smile on Adam, who had the poor grace to shake his head and say, "Oh, no, thanks. I don't do caffeine."

It was all Griff could do to keep from laughing out loud. Joan couldn't face the morning without her coffee, and she was partial to a cup of hot tea in the afternoon, too. *Strike two,* he thought. *One more and you're out, buddy.* Joan murmured something about checking on dinner and left them. Escaped, Griff told himself.

He made more small talk with the principal, beginning with his knee and going on to detail every injury he'd ever had. Adam had some suggestions to make about "staying in shape" and "targeting problem areas." Griff constantly suppressed the need to snigger. Obviously the man was a health nut and considered himself a prime specimen, even though he'd probably never done a day's physical labor or taken a genuine risk in his life. Griff listened politely to all his theories and concentrated on not letting his smile become a grin.

When Joan returned to announce that dinner was ready, Griff pulled himself up by his crutch and signaled for Adam to precede him into the dining room. Joan had set a pretty table, complete with one of Frankie's silk flower arrangements. Griff made his way without hesitation to the head of the table, first pulling out a side chair for Joan. She shot him a murderous glance as she sank down into it, but he bestowed a patient smile on her and went on his way. Adam took the spot at the opposite end of the table. Griff spread his napkin on his lap and bowed his head, his forearms braced on either side of his plate. Joan, who had been scrupulous about speaking a blessing over the evening meal, cleared her throat. Griff looked up, eyebrows lifted, but his gaze skipped over Joan and settled on Adam.

"Oh, uh, *we* always give thanks," he informed the man, who abruptly bowed his head. Griff grinned, even as Joan burned him with her eyes.

"Griff," she said sweetly, obviously paying him back, "why don't *you* say grace tonight?"

Well, it was no less than he deserved, he supposed. He bowed his head and closed his eyes, silently apologizing to God for his unfamiliarity with the task. "Lord," he said, "thank You for this good woman and her little girl. You know what they've done for me, what they mean to me. Thank You, too, for this food and, um..." He couldn't bring himself to name Adam Miller, so he finished with, "all our friends. Oh, and Lord, bless Your man Bolton and his family, especially that little baby. Amen." He lifted his head and said, "Pass the chicken, please," and unless he was mistaken, there was a smile lurking behind that amber gaze. Thirty minutes later, Griff put down his fork, touched his napkin to his mouth and said with a wink, "You've outdone yourself tonight, sugar. That was wonderful."

She narrowed her eyes at him, but murmured, "Thanks," before turning her attention to their guest. "Can I get you anything else, Adam? Would you like a slice of that wonderful fruit pie now?"

"Yes, thank you, I would," he said, switching his gaze to Griff. "What about you, Griff? Leave room for dessert?"

Griff shook his head. "Not me, but you go ahead." He looked at Joan, saying deliberately, "Darlin', did you make some coffee? I could sure use a cup."

He thought for a moment that she'd swallow her tongue, so great was her anger and her struggle to master it, but finally she managed a smile. "I won't be a moment," she trilled sweetly, adding softly, "Behave yourself," as she picked up his plate.

He drowned his need to chuckle with a swig of iced tea and fixed Adam with a hard gaze. Adam wasn't about to let himself be intimidated again, however. He turned his dessert fork over and smiled to himself.

"You really ought to try dessert," he said. "It's an arrangement of cold glazed fruit on a philo dough crust. Very low fat, very low sugar."

"Oh, I'm sure it's very healthy," Griff returned, "but Jo made a chocolate cake yesterday, and I promised Danna I'd share a piece with her and her dollies later."

"How sweet," Adam said tersely. Griff just grinned. After a lengthy silence, Adam tapped the table with his fork and said, "I don't believe I've heard Joan referred to as *Jo* before."

Griff gathered up his napkin and laid it on the table. "Well, you know how it is. I usually call her Red," he divulged, grinning, "but that's a bit too private for company."

Adam Miller blanched beneath his tan. Griff watched him mull over his options and come to a decision. He smoothed his tie and leaned forward in what must have been his best principal's pose. "Let me be perfectly straight with you, Shaw," he began, glancing at the kitchen door. "I don't want to see Joan hurt, and you're not doing her any good being here."

"I wouldn't dream of hurting her," Griff said flatly, his hands balling into fists.

Adam inclined his head. "Very likely you wouldn't," he admitted. "However, that's just what you're doing."

"I'd like to know how."

Adam sat back, a smirk on his face that made Griff itch to knock the cleft out of his chin. "This is still a small town," he said. "People here expect a schoolteacher to be above reproach."

"Are you implying," Griff grated, "that Joan is not?"

"Of course not. Nevertheless, appearances must be considered," Adam said calmly. He added pointedly, "I would hate to see her suffer *professionally* because someone... misunderstood her situation here."

Griff felt a rage unlike anything he had ever before experienced. Yet, somehow, he managed to quell it as Joan swept into the room, bearing dessert plates for Adam and herself and coffee for him. He smiled stiffly as she placed the cup and saucer before him, inclining his head in thanks, then sat back and simmered as he sipped the hot brew.

For the first time that evening, someone else carried the conversation as Joan effusively praised the dessert on her plate. Griff noted, however, that she didn't finish it. Probably so dry it stuck in her craw, he decided, eying the limp fruit slices and curling crust. He noticed, too, that she kept sending him worried glances, as if wondering what he was up to. He made a concerted effort to recreate his former ebullient self but recaptured his smile and wit only after deciding that Adam Miller should not be allowed to get away with his thinly veiled threat. Griff thought about those soft hands and his obvious horror of anything that might be deemed unhealthy and knew just what he had to do. The very idea picked up his spirits, so that he was his jolly, bantering self by the time dessert and conversation were completed and Adam rose to make his departure.

Joan was behaving as if inordinately relieved, but Griff didn't allow himself to wonder what that was about. His mind was concentrated on a single, well-defined goal, just as if he was about to climb on a bull in the chute and begin the eight-second countdown to a good ride. He felt that same calm determination, the quiet confidence, the building strength, the eagerness to face the challenge, and he didn't doubt at all what he was about to do.

He followed the others into the living room, taking long, swinging strides with his crutch. Adam declined Joan's invitation to sit down. He thanked her for a fine dinner, and after a quick glance at Griff and a smug smile, he stepped up and kissed her on the forehead, his hands closing around hers. Joan seemed shocked, so much so that she didn't even bat an eye when Griff announced that he would see their guest out.

He did more than that, actually. He helped the man put on his coat, opened the door for him and followed him out. The instant the door closed behind them, Adam spoke, obviously hoping to beat Griff to the draw. Griff smiled benignly and let him rattle on. "I hope you know, Griff," the other man was saying, "that I only have Joan's welfare at heart. Otherwise I would not have pointed out to you the pitfalls in this, um, arrangement. I take a personal interest in all my teachers, of course, but Joan—I think you'll agree—is special. She deserves the very best possible opportunity to make a permanent place for herself here."

He paused and began to pull on expensive leather driving gloves. Griff supposed silently that they came with the luxury auto parked behind Joan's old station wagon.

"I pride myself on my ability to read people, Griff," the principal went on. "I see that you truly care for Joan, and that being the case, I'm sure you'll want to do the best thing for her."

"Oh, yes," Griff said lightly, speaking for the first time. "But you know, Adam, I'm a pretty good judge of people, too, and it's obvious to me that you have your eye on the little lady, that you're so determined to have her, in fact, that you'll go so far as to threaten her livelihood in order to eliminate the competition. There's just one little problem with your approach."

"Oh?"

"Yes, indeed, and I'm going to tell you what it is. Me." With that, Griff dropped his crutch, stepped forward on a surprisingly painless knee and closed his fists around the lapels of Adam Miller's expensive suit. He lifted him easily off the ground and slammed him into the side of his car. "Now," he said, holding the shocked man there, "let's be very clear about this. If Jo suffers so much as a moment of fear about her job, I'm going to come looking for you, and when I find you—and I will find you—I'm going to break every bone in your healthy body."

"You can't threaten me!" Adam gasped, his bravado undermined by the tremor in his voice.

Griff shook him, just to prove that he could, and grinned. "Why, I'm not threatening you, Adam," he said brightly. "Veiled threats are your style, not mine. Uh-uh. I'm making you a heartfelt promise, bud. You even hint that Jo's less than the kind, caring, generous, upstanding woman we both know she is and I'm going to hurt you bad. In fact, you better pray that nothing goes wrong for her, because I just love to squash bugs like you. It might be kind of hard for me to control myself, actually. I mean, a flat tire on that old heap of hers could get your face broken, see?"

His arms were beginning to weaken, and he was becoming aware of an ache in the area of his collarbone. He told himself that he was out of shape, that it was time, after all, to look to business. He set Adam on his feet and backed off, roughly brushing the wrinkles out of his lapels.

"Now then," he began, but just then the front door opened and Joan stuck her head out, a worried expression on her face.

"Everything okay?" she asked timidly.

Griff put on a smile and wrapped a companionable arm around Adam's shoulders. "Everything's fine, darlin'."

She opened the door farther and rubbed her upper arms. "It's too cold to stand out here talking," she said.

Griff nodded and hopped back, then bent to retrieve his fallen crutch. Adam smoothed his tie, lifted his chin and opened the car door. "Well, uh, thank you for...an enlightening evening," he said.

Griff clapped him on the shoulder hard enough to make him stagger. "Our pleasure, Adam," he answered heartily. "You take care now."

Adam got into his car without another word, started it up and backed out into the street. Joan went inside and closed the door, leaving Griff to wonder if she had known Adam Miller's purpose all along and if he could justify any longer the position he had put her in. He very much feared, despite the display he had just made, that it was time to go, and he knew with a sudden heavy dread that it would be the most difficult thing he had ever done.

Chapter Eight

Griff limped into the living room, using the crutch more from habit than need. It occurred to him, briefly, that he might have done away with it a week or two earlier, but instead he had clung to it, as he'd clung to his place here. He didn't want to think about either issue, afraid of what he might discover about himself.

Joan was curled up in the armchair, focusing on a public television documentary about types of lichen, a subject in which Griff felt pretty sure she had no interest whatsoever. He took a seat on the couch, laid his crutch on the floor beside it and tried to interest himself in the program. A number of comments crossed his mind. *What a fine dinner you made for us. That Adam Miller sure doesn't look like your typical elementary-school principal. That dessert looked dry and unappetizing. That pineapple sauce was something. You don't actually like that jerk, do you?* He couldn't think of anything with which he felt comfortable. He had a feeling that anything he might say that touched on Adam Miller would open a can of worms in which he wanted no part. Unfortunately it was a can that Joan seemed determined to open on her own.

"Well?" she demanded after a long, tense silence.

He pretended not to know what she was asking, pulling his unseeing gaze from the television only with reluctance. "Beg your pardon?"

She uncurled her legs and gripped the arms of the chair with white-knuckled fingers. "I said—" she shifted again, crossing her ankles "—what did you think of... Adam."

He shrugged, hitching up one shoulder, and let his gaze wander back to the television. "Typical suit," he murmured.

"What?"

The sharpness in her tone put knots in his stomach. He felt a swelling of panic, which he instantly and instinctively repressed. He dropped his pretense and faced her with as much sincerity as possible. "Adam Miller," he said precisely, "is a jerk in an overpriced suit. He hates kids, which tells me that he's in education because that's where he's able to wield the most power over the most people. And he has the hots for you."

The color drained from her face, then surged back with red fury. "That's absurd!"

"Oh? Then tell me this. Was dinner your idea or his?" Her gaze skittered away, and the knots in his stomach began to relax. "That's what I thought," he said knowingly. "So why'd you let him bully you into this?"

He knew instantly that he shouldn't have asked that last question. The expression on her face—a combination of apology and agony—turned his knots to stone and soured his dinner. He had to look away and concentrate on slowing his suddenly accelerated heartbeat. After a long moment, he passed a hand over his face and told himself that it was time to face the music.

He took a deep breath. "You knew he was going to... suggest I leave here, didn't you?"

She swallowed and stared at her hand, saying in a small voice, "He did say that might be best."

Griff leaned forward, elbows on knees. "You want me to go." He meant it to be a question, but it came out as a statement.

She lifted her chin defensively. "I imagine you'll want to be on the road again soon, anyway," she said. "You can't support yourself just sitting here day after day, and knowing you, you're bound to be bored with this sedate lifestyle."

Bored? No, he wasn't bored, not most of the time. He got up to share coffee with Joan in the mornings, saw her off to school with Danna, then picked up the place a bit, took a nap, watched a little television, and then it was time for Danna to be home again. They played and snacked and made fun out of her printing assignments, the only real homework she had. They read together. Actually, he read and she followed every word with an intensity born of a genuine thirst for knowledge. And sometimes they just sat together in the same room, Griff with his paper, Danna with her coloring book or dolls. At those times, they would both look up at intervals, smile, and go back to their separate activities.

In the evenings, it was often the same with Joan. After dinner, they sat together in the living room, he working on a crossword puzzle or watching a television program, she with papers to grade or lesson plans to finish. At odd moments, they'd find themselves staring at one another. Joan was always the first to draw away at those times. He could have looked at her forever, and sometimes he watched her surreptitiously just for the pure pleasure of it. He loved her face and the wild abundance of her fiery hair, the way she moved her hands, the flash in her eyes, the secret smile she sometimes wore. He loved the way she ate, nibbling tiny bites of food, chewing it twice as long as would seem necessary, and swallowing with such delicacy that he marveled. He loved everything about her, even her quick temper, everything except the fear that sometimes overcame her, especially if he made the slightest romantic overture. Bored? No, anything but.

"I don't want to go," he said. He could have said, *It's my house. You're living on charity here. I'm still unwell. Your daughter loves me, needs me. Whether you know it or not, you both need me!* He said instead, "Don't you understand? I don't want to go."

"One of us has to," she told him gently, firmly, not looking at him.

"Joan," he whispered.

But she didn't look at him, wouldn't look at him.

"Honey, listen. I don't want to leave you and Danna. I... I'll marry you."

She looked at him then, astonishment sending her eyes to his before she could talk herself out of it. And she laughed. She actually laughed. "That's been tried before!" she told him scathingly. "You think I'm foolish enough to fall for that twice? Why would I? Why would I?"

"I am *not* like him!" he shouted, her unfairness driving him to his feet. "I am not Dan Burton!"

"Oh? And what makes you so different?" she lashed back. "You're known for your faithfulness, your long-term relationships?"

"I never claimed—"

"Your quiet life-style? Your dependability?"

"Plenty of people have depended on me!" he argued vehemently.

"Your stability?" she jabbed. "Your concern for family? What, Griff? Give me one reason why I should want to marry you, just one!"

Because you want me as badly as I want you, he thought, but it was the wrong thing to say. He knew that much, but he was reeling so much from her attack that he couldn't think what he ought to say. In the end, he said the only other thing that came to mind. "You could love me if you'd let yourself." He wasn't prepared for her answer to that.

"Yes," she said flatly, "but I won't." She closed her eyes and whispered, "I pray that God won't let me."

He didn't know what to say to that, didn't know how to combat such emotions. Suddenly he felt tired, weak, shaky. She prayed not to love him. No wound had ever hurt worse. He bent and picked up his crutch, leaned his weight against it. For a long moment, he just stood there looking at her, but she kept her gaze stubbornly averted. It was no use. She wouldn't, couldn't believe him. But he had to say it anyway. It just wouldn't stay inside anymore.

Slowly he made his way around the coffee table and across the room to halt at her side. He seemed to ache in every joint and limb. Worse, an empty space opened inside him, a vast, lonely, yawning place that only she could reach. He wanted to touch her hair, to rub it between his fingers and fill his hands with its lively, springy lushness. He wanted to teach her with his hands and mouth and body how he really felt about her, how special she was, how much happiness she deserved. But he knew that she couldn't allow it, that she would jerk away, turn from him, and he couldn't bear that. Instead he stared, pleading silently for a look, a chance. Finally he just said it. "I'm in love with you, you know."

She didn't move, didn't look up, didn't speak. Nothing.

Pain drove him out, pain far greater than anything he had imagined. He swung out of the room in great, swift strides, each step a desperate grab for anger or disdain, anything that would lessen the pain. It didn't help. He knew why she was as she was and that all those who had come so casually before her in his life made it harder for her to accept and believe. Why, during all that time, all those nothing one-night stands, all the temporary, fun-and-games relationships, did he never dream, never understand that one day he would find her, that she was worth waiting for, that she deserved all that passion he had so callously given away to others? Why hadn't he known that he could love a woman, really love her?

When he reached his room, he flung the crutch to the floor, closed the door and bent to catch his breath, his hands braced on the side of his bed. She prayed not to love him. Well, it wasn't a private line. He knew that much, so for the second time in the same evening, he found himself praying, needing absolution for everything in his life that had made him such a poor risk, needing a miracle, a chance, a crumb of hope. When the crumb came, he seized it eagerly, gratefully. It had a name—Bolton Charles. The preacher could tell him what to do and how to do it to win the woman he loved. He had to. He just had to.

Bolton opened the door with one hand, the other cradling a pink bundle high against his diaper-draped shoulder. Obviously surprised, he stuck his head out the door and looked both ways before greeting his visitor. "Griff," he said, "good to see you without that crutch. I don't suppose you walked all the way over here, though."

Griff nodded, his hands on his hips. He was appalled to find himself breathless after what amounted to a fair stretch of the legs. Not so long ago, he could have run the eighteen blocks between his house and the reverend's without so much as breaking into a sweat. Now his sweat suit was drenched, he ached in two dozen places, especially that knee, his lungs seemed to have shrunk alarmingly and he was freezing now that he wasn't exerting himself. He accepted Bolton's invitation to come inside with relief and gratitude, trying mightily not to limp. "Sorry I didn't call first," he gasped. "Your secretary suggested it might wake the baby."

Bolton chuckled. "It might," he said wryly, "if we could ever get her to sleep. Actually, she seems to have her days and nights mixed up, so I'm trying to keep her *awake* this morning in hopes that she'll snooze when we want her to."

"Oh." Griff dried his sweaty palms on his thighs, feeling the pull of newly knitted muscle. "This isn't a good time, then."

"No, it's fine," Bolton protested. "You can help entertain our darling little dictator so her exhausted mommy can get some sleep. Want some coffee? I'm living on it for the time being."

"That would be great," Griff said. "Point the way. I'll pour for myself."

Bolton shook his head. "Clarice would scream if I let you see the dishes piled up in our kitchen sink just now. How do you take it?"

"Black."

"Fine. You hold this. I'll get the brew." With that, he plopped the baby into Griff's unsuspecting hands and walked out of the room.

Griff juggled the soft, tiny bundle for a moment, utterly terrified, but then she let out a mewing sound, stiffened and stretched, curling her back and arms and lifting an almost nonexistent chin, and he was captivated. Laughing, he carried her to a big, overstuffed chair and sat down, carefully cradling her dark head in the bend of his elbow. She squeaked and yawned, exposing pink, toothless gums before blinking open her eyes. They were very, very dark, much, he realized, like her father's. She kicked one leg and waved her arms around, then her delicate, almost featureless face screwed up and she let out a thin, heartrending wail. Griff was devastated.

"Oh, honey, no, don't! Wait! Listen now, Daddy's coming. It's all right." Instinctively he jiggled her. She crammed her fist in her mouth and sucked loudly, her eyes closing. He panicked, thinking she was about to go to sleep, and lifted her against his shoulder as Bolton had done to pat her comfortingly on her soft back. She let out a loud, smelly belch, surprising and shocking Griff, who had never expected so unladylike a sound from such a tiny female.

Bolton chuckled, coming back into the room. "Hey, you do that pretty well. Want a part-time job? Mother's helper, good with colicky babies."

Griff jiggled the newborn on his shoulder. "Might solve one of my problems," he said wryly.

Bolton set Griff's coffee cup on the side table, then sat on the couch with his own, apparently content to leave his daughter where she was.

Griff lowered the baby to his lap. She made sucking sounds and waved her fists around, her eyes wide and glued to his face. He smiled at her as he reached for his cup, bouncing his legs up and down gently when she looked as if she might wail again. This baby thing wasn't so difficult after all, he mused as her eyes crossed and she struggled to focus them again. For a moment, he imagined that this was his child, that her hair was flaming red and her eyes the color of amber. The very idea moved him almost to the point of tears, and he set his cup down again without so much as a sip.

"Want to talk about it?" Bolton prodded gently.

Griff nodded his head, took a deep breath and told him everything.

Some time later, Bolton poured Griff a fresh cup of coffee and returned to pick up his sleeping daughter from Griff's lap and stir her gently into wakefulness. She mewled and stretched and boxed her ears with unmanageable hands, then latched onto the bottle that Bolton offered her and began sucking greedily. Bolton supported her head with one steady hand and held the bottle at the right angle with the other, but his words showed that his thoughts were very much with Griff. "You could ask her to leave," he said lightly. "It might buy you some time."

Griff shook his head. "It's her home, hers and Danna's. Besides, I can't have her thinking I'm mean enough to put them out of their home and convince her I'm sincere, too."

"And you say that you told her that you love her?" Bolton asked thoughtfully.

The pain of that lanced through Griff and left him gasping for breath. "Yes."

"And you asked her to marry you?"

"Yes." But had he really? "Well..." He replayed the memory in his mind. "No, I didn't ask her to marry me. I said that I would marry her."

Bolton winced. "Big difference."

Griff sighed. "I don't know what to do or say. I've never felt so helpless."

"You might try telling her just what you've told me, that you regret your former life-style, that you love her and can't imagine a future without her or Danna, that you'll do whatever it takes to help her trust you and love you."

"It won't change anything," Griff muttered. "She could love me, she admitted that, but she *prays* not to. That's how afraid of me she is."

"It's not necessarily you, Griff," Bolton told him. "She's afraid of being hurt again. It's perfectly natural after the disaster of her first marriage. She doesn't trust her own judgment anymore."

"But it is me," Griff argued. "She had me pegged dead to rights from the beginning. I'm the very last sort of man she should get mixed up with."

"Were," Bolton said. "You *were* the very last sort of man she should get mixed up with, but that's changed now, and I don't believe it was an accident, Griff."

"What d'you mean?"

Bolton pulled the bottle from the baby's mouth, lifted her to his shoulder and patted her gently on the back. She grunted and squeaked and wobbled around like a worm on a hook, but she didn't burp. Bolton kept automatically patting, the action seemingly ingrained after only a couple weeks of experience. "Do you suppose it's coincidence, Griff, that the one woman in the world who could make you want to change just happened to be living in your house at the very time you were forced back there?"

"I hadn't thought of it like that," Griff admitted.

"How many bulls have you ridden without being seriously hurt?"

Griff shrugged. "Hundreds, thousands, more likely."

"Have you ever known Frankie to spend the winter in Florida before?"

"No. Or anywhere else for that matter, but I haven't exactly been living in her pocket."

"Still, it's unusual. And what about her 'accident'? Now I'm not saying that God made her fall, broke her hip to keep her out of the way, but it was awfully coincidental—provided you believe in coincidence, and I'm not at all sure that I do."

Griff thought it over and came up with, "So what you're saying is that Jo and I are meant to be together."

Bolton smiled. "Something like that."

Griff felt the same warm, hopeful feeling that had overtaken him the evening before. They were meant to be. Surely that would count for something. Surely she would see it, too. He leaned forward expectantly, elbows on knees, determined not to blow this one chance at what was meant to be. "Okay," he said, "but what if I can't convince her?"

Bolton smiled and thrust the baby at him. "Here, you seem to have a knack for this."

Awkwardly Griff put the baby against his shoulder and patted her between her delicate shoulder blades. His hand, it seemed, was heavier than the minister's. He made a concerted effort to lighten his strokes, but his mind was occupied with other matters. The force of his hand increased, not enough to harm the baby, but more than one would consciously use with an infant. After several sturdy whacks, little Melanie burped a loud, milky bubble up out of her stomach.

Bolton crossed his legs and smiled. "Ah, so that's the secret!" he said with satisfaction. Griff simply blinked at him. Bolton sobered, or at least made a valiant attempt at it. "As for your question, Griff, I think you'll find a way. I think you've got what it takes to do what you ought. In fact, I'm quite sure of it."

"Let's hope so," Griff said, patting the baby affectionately. "Now how do I go about it?"

Bolton sobered then and gave it to him in a nutshell. "Patience and honesty, Griff. Patience and honesty—and faith."

* * *

"Oh, she's adorable!" Joan gushed.

Clarice Charles smiled. "We think so. Griff does, too."

Joan immediately stiffened. "Griff?"

Clarice nodded, her gaze penetrating. "Mmm, hmm, I walked in here this morning—stumbled in, really, after a much-needed nap—and found him giving her a bottle. He burped her, too. No small feat, believe me. Bolton says he's a natural, and he would know. He's such a wonderful father himself."

"You're very lucky," Joan murmured, wondering how Griff had managed a visit to the Charles home.

"Blessed," Clarice corrected lightly. "I'm very blessed, not lucky. There's a difference, you know."

"Hmm? Oh, of course."

Clarice's smile was slightly mocking. "I'm so glad," she said. "Some people never get it, and then they miss out."

"Miss out?" Joan echoed uncertainly.

"On the blessings in store for them."

Joan wasn't feeling as though she had any blessings in store, only dangers, threats to the peaceful existence she had built for herself and her daughter. Danna was the only blessing she could see, and everything else was difficulty and danger. She had been robbed even of much of her enjoyment in her work. Adam Miller had been distinctly cool to her today, even short, and she feared what was to come. He was her superior after all, and apparently Griff was right about his having some interest in her personally. While she was relieved to have that interest derailed, she couldn't help feeling that in doing so, Griff had dealt her an even more difficult hand to play.

She could have handled the principal's personal overtures, but she was at his mercy as far as her work situation was concerned. He could make things very difficult for her.

He could make things impossible for her. And she had Griff to thank for that, never mind that she had introduced the two by cravenly allowing Adam to try to dislodge her unwelcome housemate. But then, it was his house after all. Oh, if only she could be free of him! Somehow she must get free of him.

She dismissed her curiosity about his visit with the Charleses and proffered the gift that had served as her excuse to show up on their doorstep. "It isn't much," she apologized in advance, "but I hope you'll like it."

"Oh, I'm sure we will," Clarice told her. "Here, we'll trade. You take the baby and I'll unwrap the gift, all right?"

"Wonderful," Joan said, reaching for the baby. She really was a tiny thing, despite the chubby cheeks and folds about her wrists. She had her father's hair and her mother's nose, but that could change, of course. Joan cradled her close and spoke quietly to her in the tone of voice that had always soothed Danna at this age. But this sleepy little lady did not share Danna's exuberance. All she wanted was a nap. Danna's natural curiosity had kept her awake in the daytime. The need for sleep could not compete with the need to see and hear and experience. The struggle with Danna had been to calm her, to temper that natural enthusiasm with discipline and serenity. She felt, all in all, that she had done a good job. She had learned, like every other parent, by trial and error. It seemed a shame, in some ways, to let all that experience go to waste. There ought to be another child to benefit from that dearly earned wisdom. But there would not. There couldn't be. She had resigned herself to that long ago.

She thought she had gotten over that sadness. Danna, after all, ought to be enough for any parent, and yet... Joan lifted the infant close to her face and inhaled the peculiar perfume of baby, catching in the process the whiff of ammonia that signaled a wet diaper.

Aching nostalgia swept over her. She would never know what it meant to hold her own newborn again, because she would never know what it meant to make love with a man again. She couldn't. She didn't dare. The risks were entirely too great. She couldn't survive a second heartbreak like the first. She smiled at Clarice Charles, hoping the sparkle in her eyes would be mistaken for anything other than what it was. "I think we need a dry diaper."

Clarice instantly set aside the half-opened gift. "Naturally! We won't be a minute."

"No, let me," Joan protested. "Is her diaper bag around anywhere?"

"By the door," Clarice said, getting up. "We've learned to keep it there to remind us not to leave without it! How quickly we forget these little essentials, though in my case maybe it's understandable. It's been nine years since I last dealt with a newborn." She shook her head as she carried the diaper bag back to Joan's place on the couch. "So many wasted years," she said, her eyes locking with Joan's.

A message? Joan wondered. She didn't want to know. She took the items Clarice dug out of the bag and turned her attention to changing Miss Melanie's britches while Clarice resumed opening the gift. Clarice was done before Joan. She cried out in delight at the small fabric angel with the clip to attach it to the baby's clothing and the elastic tether for her pacifier.

"Her very own guardian angel," Clarice said. "How appropriate!"

Joan smiled. "I thought so. As I said, it isn't very much, but—"

"Oh, stop it," Clarice interrupted firmly. "We know your circumstances are delicate—a single mother with a traditionally low paying job. We've never counted our friends dear by the price of their gifts. It would be horribly hypocritical of us. We aren't exactly wealthy ourselves, you know. But another year or two, and we'll be a two-income family, not that that will put us over the top, either. I'll be doing what you are."

"Teaching? Really? I knew you had been attending college until this last semester, but I didn't realize you were an education major."

Clarice nodded as Joan pulled Melanie's pink sleeper into place and began fastening the snaps. "I'm going to give myself one more semester off, then start in again in the summer," she said.

"Well," Joan told her, "you'll be needing a sitter then, I suppose. Maybe we can work something out. Just for the summer, you understand."

"What a wonderful idea!" Clarice exclaimed. "Unless . . . circumstances do change."

"Mine won't," Joan said flatly, lifting the baby into her arms again. "That is, I suppose we'll have to move in the spring." She busied herself talking nonsense to the baby, who screwed up her face in what could have been a smile but probably wasn't.

Clarice said nothing for some time, just curled her legs beneath her and watched. "Would you like to speak to my husband?" she asked finally. "I'll wake him, if you want."

Joan kept her gaze averted, but shook her head. "I wouldn't dream of depriving him of his sleep. It isn't important, really."

Clarice sat forward suddenly. "Maybe you could tell me."

For some reason, that offer moved Joan almost to tears. She had no intention of taking her up on it, of course, but somehow she heard herself saying, "I want him to go. He has to go! It's just impossible now. I can't stand it anymore! And it's not fair. It's just not fair!" The tears she had fought so successfully before began streaming down her face.

Clarice got up and moved to sit beside her. She took the baby from her and laid the little one snugly in the corner of the couch before wrapping an arm around Joan's shoulders. "You're in love with him," she said succinctly.

Joan could not have been more horrified. "No! I would never... fall in love with a man like Griff Shaw. I know his type so well! It—it's just the opposite, in fact. I can't abide him. That's why I want him gone!"

Clarice smoothed the distraught woman's hair with a gentle hand and said almost apologetically, "You sound like I did not so long ago. My great fears were being controlled and failing to live up to expectations. When love came, it panicked me. But my husband's a wise and patient man, and he didn't let me deny my feelings for him."

Joan dried her face and calmed herself. "Griff Shaw," she said, "is not Bolton Charles."

"No, he isn't," Clarice agreed, "but he might be just the man you need."

Joan laughed, but it wasn't from humor. "Hardly. He's just exactly the type of man I *don't* need."

"Type?" Clarice echoed lightly. "Is that really fair, Joan? Don't we all have the right to be taken on our own terms?"

"You don't understand," Joan told her stubbornly.

"I think I do," Clarice argued mildly, "but we'll let that go. I'll tell you what I know. Griff was here this morning to talk to Bolton about you. The conversation, of course, is privileged, but I don't think I'll be betraying anybody's confidence when I tell you that Griff is in love with you."

Joan sprang to her feet, controlling the surge of anger she felt only with great difficulty. "I've heard that one before," she said cryptically. "Honestly, how can you be so taken in by him?"

Clarice folded her hands and sighed before turning to lift her napping daughter into wakefulness. She stood with the baby and smiled patiently. "Don't let fear rob you of the blessings meant for you, Joan," she said softly. "Take what God offers with both hands, and a goodly dose of faith wouldn't hurt, either."

"I know you're trying to help," Joan said, "but...I know what I have to do."

Clarice smiled thoughtfully. "Yes, maybe you do at that," she mused and seized Joan's hand, squeezing it affectionately. "Whatever happens, we'll be here for you, always."

Joan returned her clasp impulsively. "Thank you," she whispered, but she promised herself that their support would not be needed. She simply would not allow it to be. She couldn't.

Chapter Nine

"You're leaving."

The relief in her voice made him grit his teeth, but he pushed the ache and irritation aside and turned to face her. "Yes."

She leaned against the doorframe, trying to look nonchalant. "Why?"

He shook his head and turned away again. "I have things to do."

"What sort of things?"

"Does it matter?"

She didn't answer, just stared at him with enormous, ambivalent eyes. He went on packing his bag. She was so quiet and still that for a moment he thought she had left, but then he heard the subtle swishing of fabric and the scraping of leather against carpet that signaled a shift in her weight, and he smiled to himself.

"You went to the Charleses today."

His smile grew broader, but he didn't turn around. "Yes."

"I—I went to see the baby, and Clarice told me you'd been there. I was wondering...I mean, she said you walked there."

He continued putting his things into the bag, one at a time. "Mmm, hmm. Jogged most of the way, actually."

"Wasn't that a bit ill-advised?"

His knee was throbbing even then, but it was endurable. He had lived with worse. The weakness, however, could not be borne. "Have to start somewhere," he said lightly.

"You could have walked around the block. You didn't have to go all the way there."

"I had a few things to talk over with the preacher."

"Oh."

He heard the unasked question and ignored it.

Another long silence passed before she asked, "Where will you go?"

He shrugged. "Motel, I suppose."

"Can you afford that?" she asked softly.

Here we go, he thought. He took a deep breath, picked up a bankbook from the bed and turned around. "Here." She took it gingerly from his outstretched hand, confusion and curiosity mingled on her face. She thumbed through it warily. As she took in the amounts recorded there, her eyebrows began to float upward and her jaw began to drop. He reached behind him and picked up another with a navy blue cover. "That's the savings account. You're welcome to the checking."

She snatched it out of his hand, shook it open to the final entry and glanced at the figures. Then she threw it at him. "You lied to me!"

The bankbook fluttered harmlessly to the floor at his feet. He put his hands to his hips and swung his weight onto his uninjured leg. "Yep."

"Why?"

He knew it was an explanation he didn't really have to make, but he made it anyway. "I wanted to stay. You didn't want me to."

"So you lied!"

"So I lied."

She threw the savings book this time. It flew past his head and plopped on the floor on the opposite side of the bed. He ignored it and went after her instead. He caught her arm between the wrist and the elbow just as she whirled through the door.

"Let go of me!"

He hauled her back into the room, slipped around her and closed the door, keeping himself between her and it.

"How dare you!"

"As usual," he said, "you don't give me much choice."

"Damn you!"

"Maybe, but not for this." He saw the desperation in her eyes, but it didn't cushion the blow he felt at her next words.

"I hate you!"

He was suddenly angry and striding toward her. "Now who's lying?" She reeled as if he'd hit her. He made himself stop and swallow down the anger, made himself remember that he was at least partly at fault, made himself acknowledge his mistakes. He leveled his shoulders and stilled his heartbeat by sheer will, much as he did in the moment before that gate opened and he burst into the arena astride a mountain of bucking, stomping, twisting, ripping, snorting bull. "You were right," he said, shaking his head. "Oh, man, you had me pegged dead to rights."

She drew her brows together, glancing alertly from side to side. "What do you mean?"

He sighed. "It was all part of the game at first."

"What game?"

"The Get-Red-into-Bed game."

Her face suddenly clashed with her hair.

"I know what you're thinking," he said, "but that's the point. It had all changed by Christmas Eve. I changed. I...got tired of the game. It wasn't enough anymore."

"Wasn't enough," she whispered. "So you're going?"

He nodded. "But don't think you've gotten rid of me."

She blinked at him. "I...I don't understand you."

He folded his arms. "Maybe not, but you need me. Whether you know it or not, you need me."

She started to shake her head, caught herself and dropped her gaze. "Danna—"

"Needs me," he finished for her, hooking his thumbs into the waistband of his jeans. She straightened abruptly and opened her mouth as if to take issue, but he dropped his bomb first. "I want to adopt her."

"A-a-a-a..."

He thought she might fall down. He grabbed her by the shoulders and walked her to the foot of the bed. He sat her down and started clearing away the remaining items scattered across the bed by stuffing them hurriedly into the bag. Finished, he shoved the bag aside, then bent, picked up the one bankbook and laid it atop the bag. He sat down beside her and waited. He could tell by the way her eyes were working back and forth that she was truly considering his suggestion. Finally she looked at him.

"Why would you want to adopt her?"

"I want to be her father," he said.

"But—"

"I know, if it doesn't work out between us, it'll be a mess, but that doesn't change how I feel about her."

"I can't let you—"

"You don't really think I'd take her away from you, do you?"

"I don't..." She blinked her eyes rapidly as if waking up from a dream. "This is absurd."

He laid his hand over hers. "No, it isn't. She loves me, and I love her."

She snatched her hand away. "She's a five-year-old!"

"Who needs a daddy."

"And you're volunteering?"

He chuckled. "More like I've been drafted, if you ask me." He lowered his voice to help her understand. "I didn't choose to love either one of you. It just happened. I'm trying to deal with it as best I can. You'll have to do the same."

She bounced up to her feet. "I don't *have* to do anything."

"Oh, yes, you do, for Danna's sake if no one else's."

He saw the truth of that wash over her. "But adoption—"

"Takes a long time," he said. "I want to get started. If we get to the wedding first, well, so much the better."

"Wedding?" she gasped.

He ignored that. "I never thought of myself as a patient man," he said, "but I'm learning. Still and all, whatever happens with you and me—"

"*Nothing* is going to happen—"

"I'm still gonna be here for that little girl."

"—between you and me!"

"So you might as well get used to it." They glared at one another for a full minute before he sighed and shook his head. "Dadgummit, I've missed so much already. When I was holding that little baby today, I thought, 'Danna was this small once, and I never got to hold her like this.' Doesn't seem fair somehow, but you ride what you draw."

Joan's eyes grew large again. "You're serious about this!"

"I'm serious about all of it, and I'm not going away. Period."

"You can't just push your way into our lives!" she exclaimed.

"Guess I can," he said. "I have. And you can't push me out again."

"And why not?"

"Because, darlin', when push comes to shove, I've got all the power on my side. I figured it out, see. The world's full of men who'd just love to slide between the sheets with you, but you're only scared of *me.*"

"Because you're the one pressuring me!" she retorted.

He shook his head. "Because I'm the one you want."

Her mouth dropped open, and he saw the panic that shimmered brightly in her eyes, but then she pulled that old shield into place, and Red was back, temper and all. "Of all the arrogant, conceited, insulting*...men!*"

He couldn't help grinning. He loved that fire in her. "Like our fingerprints, darlin', we're all different. That's one lesson you still haven't learned."

"And you're going to teach me, I suppose!"

"Not me. As far as I'm concerned, I'm the only man you have any need to figure out, and starting today, I have no secrets."

"Oh, right, and if I believe that, you've got a bridge you want to sell me!"

"What I want," he said patiently, "is to love you and live with you for the rest of my life. What I want is to be a husband and a daddy, your husband, Danna's daddy—and maybe someone else's, too, from the beginning this time."

"In your dreams, cowboy."

"But I'm a man who goes after his dreams, Red."

She folded her arms, eyes narrowed. "You'll do anything to get what you want, won't you?"

He canted his head slightly. "You can't paint me with Dan Burton's brush, Jo, not anymore."

She thrust her shoulders back and took another shot. "If you think I'd marry some fly-by-his-pants rodeo bum, whatever his bankbook says, you've got another think coming!"

He leaned back, elbows locked, upper body weight levered against his arms, hands planted in the mattress. He grinned. "What rodeo bum would that be, sugar?"

Those amber eyes flashed fire. "Don't expect me to believe you'd give up the rodeo!"

"Not give it up exactly, just go at it from a different angle."

"As if that would make a difference."

"It might."

"Not with me."

His grin softened into a smile. "We'll see."

She stared for a moment, and then she threw up her hands. "Fine, so long as your leaving."

"Leaving, not disappearing. I'll be here when Danna gets home from school tomorrow afternoon."

A look of alarm overcame her, and suddenly she was shaking a finger at him. "You are not to say anything about adoptions or weddings to my daughter!"

He lifted a brow at that and rose to his feet. "Are you suggesting I lie to the child, Joan?" he asked, stepping forward.

She started backing away. "N-no, just don't mention it!"

"Lies of omission," he said, shaking his head and going slowly after her. "She has a right to know."

"She's five years old!"

"She's got just as much at stake in this family as the rest of us."

"What family?" she scoffed.

"*Our* family," he said gently.

She backed up against the door and rapped her head smartly against it. Her hand flew up to check for bumps. "We—we don't have a family."

"We will."

She rubbed her head and smirked, turning his own words back at him. "We'll see."

He braced his hands on either side of her head. "That's right, hot stuff, and I won't even say that I told you so."

She rolled her eyes, but as he stepped closer he noted other things with deep satisfaction, things like the flare of nostrils picking up a heady scent, like the suddenly accelerated pulse beat at the base of her throat, the quickened breathing, the stillness of expectation. Signs of desire. For him. He wanted to drag her over to the bed and take his fill, but he wanted the giving more, the loving. At last he knew the difference, and so would she, God willing, so would she.

He nudged her nose gently with his, then moved to her temple and breathed heat into her ear. She shivered and pressed herself against the door. He smiled and drew back a few inches to stare down at her. "Scared?" he whispered.

She was terrified, and he knew it, but she lifted her chin defiantly. "Of—of what?"

"This." He brushed his mouth over hers. She parted her lips expectantly, then abruptly turned her face away. He settled for the hollow just behind her ear, her glorious hair teasing him as he slid the tip of his tongue down the pale column of her neck. He heard the sharp intake of her breath and the beginning of the moan that she throttled into silence. He wanted that moan, and he got it. He bit her and sucked her flesh into his mouth. She was sweet, sweet as candy and hot as red pepper.

Suddenly her hands were on his shoulders, but whether to push him away or draw him closer, he didn't wait to discover. He captured her mouth in a clash of tongues and threw his body against hers, pinning her to the door. Her arms went around his neck. He brought his hands to her face and tilted it so that he could plumb the depths of her mouth. She wasn't fighting him. Just the opposite, in fact. Rather quickly, she was all over him, arms—and legs—winding around him almost feverishly, and he knew he had to stop, now, while he still could.

He broke the kiss and laid his forehead against hers, trying to calm the clamorings of his body. After several moments, he worked enough space between them that she had to get her feet on the floor or fall. When he was certain she was steady, he pulled away entirely. She was angry, and he didn't blame her.

"What's the matter, Griff? Isn't that what you want?"

He looked her straight in the eye. "Oh, it's part of what I want," he admitted raggedly, "but sex alone is not enough anymore, Red, not for me and not for you, no matter what you're thinking now."

"What I'm thinking now," she snapped, "is that I can't get away from you fast enough!"

He sighed, wishing he could spare them both what was to come, but like he'd told the preacher, whatever it took. "Baby," he promised gently, "you can't get away from me at all. You're mine. You're always going to be mine, and the sooner you get used to the idea, the sooner we can all be just what we're supposed to be."

"And that is?" she demanded.

"Happy," he said simply, "and together."

"The two are mutually exclusive," she insisted sourly, her bottom lip trembling even as she lashed out in anger. "*I'll* be happy just as soon as you're gone!" She was so happy, in fact, that she tore from the room in sobs.

He wanted to go after her, but he knew it would do no good. She needed time, Bolton had said, to learn to trust again. When she learned to trust her own feelings and her own judgment, she would be ready to trust him. Now all he had to do was stay the course. He walked around the bed and picked up the other bankbook, slowly straightened and slid it into his bag. He closed the bag, hoisted it onto his shoulder with hardly a twinge of pain and carried it around the bed to the dresser, where he'd left his hat. With one hand he picked it up by the crown and fitted it onto his head. He didn't have to look in the mirror to know when he'd gotten it just right. He could tell by the feel of it, without even thinking about it—and he wasn't thinking about it.

He was thinking about the moment when he could finally take her in his arms and know it was going to be all right, about a home, a real home, that Jo could call her own, about Danna's first horse, and a baby that got her days and nights mixed up. Heck, two or three maybe, stair-stepped redheads! He was thinking about sitting down to a busy dinner table in a warm kitchen, about slamming doors and little voices ringing out, "I'm home!" He was thinking about hugs and sloppy kisses—and having Red in his bed. Every night. For the rest of his life. He was thinking about church on Sundays and Thanksgiving here at Frankie's, about in-laws and outlaws, friends who wouldn't understand. He was thinking of skinned knees and lost teeth and Jo's belly growing big with his kid.

The world of bars and buckle bunnies, high rides and low roads, drinking and dancing and charming his way into beds he had no business being in, hangovers and hanging out,

always moving on, those old days, that old life, seemed dir
and far away. Empty. Pointless. He wouldn't be going bac
to that again, whatever happened. He hardly knew the ma
he had been, but he knew the man he wanted to be, was go
ing to be. He turned around and strode swiftly from th
room on a painful knee, leaving behind the woman he love
so that she could find her own way to that place where the
could both be what they should.

It wasn't working. He was as much with them as if he wa
still living in the house. He was there most afternoons whe
she came home from work, a look of longing in his eyes s
intense that she couldn't bear to see it. She shouldn't hav
allowed the arrangement to stand, but Danna couldn't com
home to an empty house, and he was saving her money o
baby-sitters. Besides, Danna would have been bitterly dis
appointed if she'd had to spend her afternoons with any
one else.

True, they didn't stay home very much. Griff always ha
somewhere to go and something to do. "Business," h
would say, but what kind of business was another ques
tion. When she asked, he talked about looking at some
one's "operation," several someones, actually. Danna wa
no more helpful. She would say they went to the bank. The
went to some office. They had coffee and soda with this on
and that one. They looked at a horse. They looked at stock
They talked to Grandma Frankie on the phone. The
bought a truck, a great deal of truck, a double cab dual axl
truck in fire-engine red, the very make and model Joan ha
recommended. The vanity license plate he ordered read
RDO BUM, and Danna helped him attach it to the front o
the truck just above the big shiny chrome bumper.

Joan read about the purchase of the ranch in the news
paper before Danna thought to say anything to her. Grif

Shaw was big news all by himself around Duncan. The purchase of a sizable chunk of the surrounding countryside made for front-page coverage. She read that he was setting up a specialized ranching operation and a school of some sort, though he denied that he was retiring, just "coming at it from another angle," as he'd told her. This reprioritizing of his career and life had nothing to do directly with the injuries he'd received in last year's finals, he claimed. It was, instead, a matter of it being time to settle down, act like a grown-up and be a "real man." He would say nothing further about the possibility of a certain someone having stolen his heart, but the writer could report that there had been several confirmed sightings about town of the champion bull rider in company with a ravishing young redhead. The article was accompanied by a picture of a smiling Danna in full cowgirl regalia standing next to a crouching Griff Shaw, her arm wrapped around his neck. It was a toss-up as to who wore the biggest smile.

Joan felt in some ways like a noose was slowly closing around her neck, but Griff himself was applying no pressure. Nevertheless, he was there too much, always smiling, always hoping, and ever ready to talk about one matter or another. How was her work? Her sister and parents? Shouldn't he get someone to fix that leaky faucet in the powder room? What did she think about having a garage door opener installed? He happened to think Frankie would appreciate it. He was always talking to Frankie these days, too, and reporting those conversations dutifully, especially when Frankie decided that it was time to head for home. She was expected any day now, but Joan was not to feel that she must leave the house. Frankie would welcome the company and the help for some time to come yet. When the day came to leave, he'd make sure that she had a place to go to, a place that fully met all her needs. She told him flatly that she could find her own place, meet her own needs, but she se cretly felt relief and an odd confidence that he would d exactly as he said.

There were some matters so disturbing, however, tha Joan's temper let fly. For one thing, he wanted to giv Danna an allowance. It was a pittance, a dollar and a half week, but it was the principle of the matter that got Joan' dander up. She was Danna's parent, not Griff. He calme her, placated her and dropped the matter, but Danna be came quietly and smoothly employed in a number of sma ways, so that a buck here and a buck there found their wa into her pockets. She hauled off sticks or moved rocks c sponged the fronts of the kitchen cabinets. Joan bit her li and looked the other way. But then he announced that h wanted to buy Danna a horse and teach her to ride it.

For once Joan was able to come down foursquare agains something and make it stick. Griff was not to give he daughter a horse. A horse was a great, hulking, dangerou thing, far too expensive to accept as a gift from a "friend, emphasis on friend. It required enormous upkeep and wa much too difficult to be cared for by a mere five-year-olc who was too small and too young to even consider learnin to ride. She absolutely forbade him to give Danna a horse on threat of restricting their contact on grounds of endan germent on his part. Griff quickly and humbly backed dow after arguing briefly that five-year-olds the world over we regularly mounting up. The matter was closed, and Joan fe a certain satisfaction in having won a decisive battle. Grif turned his attention to other things.

The ranch came with a small but livable house, whic Griff had immediately moved into and furnished with th essentials. Danna helped him pick out a "can of peas" be for the "extra" room. At Danna's urging, Joan decided tha she had to see that "extra" room. It was clearly a little girl' room, complete with a white French provincial bed with a lacy ruffled canopy and matching bedspread. Danna was as happy and proud of that room as if it were her own, and Joan had no doubts that that was exactly Griff's intention. The argument she prepared about it didn't come off as she'd planned, however. When she blasted him for decorating the room in such a manner, he confessed a lamentable lack of personal expertise when it came to domestic matters such as making a home and promptly asked her advice.

Quite before she knew what was happening, they'd spent an hour debating whether or not to go with a Southwestern theme throughout or a more jumbled, homey mix of styles. Griff was even thinking of knocking out a wall and building on or maybe just starting from scratch and building a brand-new dream house. Joan thought it would be a shame to waste what he already had, especially after he'd outfitted the kitchen with top-of-the-line appliances and put in central air. Plus, there were some wonderful old trees around the place that he wouldn't want to lose and the view from the narrow front porch would be spectacular once spring was in full bloom. They decided which wall should go and what needed to be built on, then decided that it would be best to do it in stages. He wanted a fireplace and a lot more porches right away and a whirlpool in the new bathroom he was planning. She told him that closets were more important. Not a one in the place was truly adequate! He scrawled "closets" at the top of the list he was preparing for the contractor, and her frustration at failing to engage him in the planned battle diminished in the face of pure enjoyment and a certain unidentified longing.

After that, she tried to pull back. She arranged play dates for Danna after school. She had mysterious "other plans" when he wanted to take them out to dinner. But not an evening passed when Danna wasn't on the phone with Griff two or three times. Sometimes they talked while they watched the same television program, just as if they were in the room together, and they talked about her. Griff always asked about her, and Danna always answered openly and forthrightly. Mommy was "fine" or "working papers" or "a little sad."

The night she had the awful headache, Danna called Griff with the news and he was there in twenty minutes, a worried look on his face, a bottle of analgesics in hand. He insisted on giving her a neck rub, saying that she had nursed him and it was only fair that he return the favor. While she lay beneath a blanket on the couch with a cool cloth on her forehead, he put Danna to bed, then dimmed the lights, turned on some soothing music and sat with her pounding head in his lap until she drifted off to sleep. She woke the next morning feeling wonderful, curled up beneath the blanket, her head pillowed on his thigh. He'd sat up all night rather than disturb her.

She couldn't concentrate on her work that day or seem to sleep that next night for wondering if he'd changed as much as he seemed to have or if he'd always been such a thoughtful, caring person without anyone on whom to focus those traits. But then, she told herself, there had always been Frankie, and he hadn't exactly showered her with attention. On the other hand, he'd built her a fine home and apparently seen to her every financial need along the way. And weren't adults supposed to separate emotionally to a degree from those who reared them? She didn't exactly live next door to her mother. She couldn't very well do that and live her own life. Then again, she had never lived the sort of life that Griff Shaw had. *Had,* she was forced to admit, being the operative word—or so it seemed.

Then came the rodeo. Griff stopped by the house very early one morning with notebook in hand. He had mapped out a schedule of all the top rides across the country, eight before the end of the year, "providing the kneeholds." Joan couldn't believe her ears. It was proof positive, she shouted at him, that he had not changed and never would. He tried to explain that he had to keep his hand in until the riding school was well established. After all, how could he teach the fine art of bull riding to all those potential young champions if he didn't keep his technique polished? Why would they even want—or pay for—his help if he lost that edge? And what about Danna, she wanted to know? How could he just fly off to some rodeo somewhere when he knew that she'd be expecting to see him when she got off the school bus every day? When he explained that he'd already talked it over with Danna and that she understood, Joan went ballistic.

How dared he take it upon himself to talk over anything with her daughter? Who did he think he was? What right did he have to insinuate himself into their lives like this and then worm his way back out again? During all the shouting, Danna came in, rubbing her eyes and looking frightened. When she asked shakily what was wrong, both Griff and Joan instantly sought to reassure her. Then, to Joan's horror, she watched her daughter walk, not into her arms, but into Griff Shaw's! Within moments, she had reduced both her daughter and herself to tears with her sharp, irrational tongue. She might have done real and permanent harm if Griff hadn't taken matters into his own hands. While she ranted at him, he swung Danna up onto his hip, stalked across the room, reached out with one hand, clamped it around the back of her neck and hauled her up to him.

"Lady," he said through clenched teeth, "if I didn't love you and understand where all this nonsense was coming from, I'd walk out now and never come back, but the fact is, I do, so I won't, but you're pushing it. You're sure pushing it."

"What's wrong, cowboy?" she sniped. "I thought when push came to shove, *you* had all the power."

"And so I do," he told her with a grin, and just to prove it, he kissed her full on the mouth, right there with Danna riding his hip and giggling behind her hand. It was no quick thing, either, that kiss, but the staking of a claim, the branding of his property, the ending of any argument. When it was over, he kissed Danna on the forehead, told her he'd see her that afternoon, let her down and walked out, leaving his notebook on the table.

Flustered and not a little pleased despite the indignation she tried to fan back to life, Joan glossed over the incident as best she could before sending her daughter upstairs to get dressed for school. She poured herself a second cup of coffee and sat down at the table, muttering about the fickleness of the male gender in general and a certain cowboy in particular, but she couldn't seem to concentrate on her invective with that notebook lying there in plain sight. Telling herself that if he didn't want her to look in it, he shouldn't have left it behind, she drew it to her and began to flip through the pages.

It was more than a notebook, actually. It was a planner similar to the one she used when mapping out the school year. In it, Griff had noted all the highest-paying rodeos, then circled the dates for Danna's birthday, her own, his and Frankie's, as well as Mother's Day, Father's Day, Thanksgiving and the whole month of December. That meant he had ruled out beforehand the national finals entirely.

He really was pulling back, paring down his schedule in order to be home at all the most important times, cutting back so much that he'd have no shot at the national championship, for which only the top money winners of the year were allowed to compete. He'd cut himself out of the money, while still managing to keep his name up there before the fans and the public. In other words, he was doing exactly what he claimed to be doing—keeping his hand in just enough to draw paying students to his riding school. A bull-riding school. Joan shook her head, feeling fresh tears pooling in her eyes.

Oh, why was he doing this to her? To him? She wasn't worth it. He'd see, eventually, that she wasn't worth it. She was all challenge and no reward because she couldn't love him. She didn't dare love him. Did she?

She was convinced now, thumbing through that notebook, that he was sincere, that he was turning himself around and building a life he could share with a wife and a family. *"What I want is to love you and live with you for the rest of my life. What I want is to be a husband and a daddy, your husband, Danna's daddy—and maybe someone else's, too, from the beginning this time."* For one moment, she let herself think about it, dream about it—being married to and loved by Griff Shaw, making a family and a home with him, making a baby with him. Could it really happen? Could they—she—really make him happy enough to stay?

The possibility of failure was just too strong, though, too frightening. She pushed those scary thoughts aside and began nervously flipping through the pages of the book, when she spied a block of dates outlined in red. She stopped and smoothed the page. July. The week of the Fourth of July. A rodeo in Independence, Missouri. He had written in the words, "The whole family. Rothman's Candy House, Dillard's Pizza, Westward Ho! Fireworks!" He was describing a working holiday for the family, *their* family, planning to show them all the great places he had discovered there during previous visits. He was planning a whole wonderful life for them, and she didn't know if she had the courage to reach out and take it. But she wanted to. She wanted it so badly that she could taste it. And she hated Griff Shaw for making her want it. She hated him—and she loved him. So much that it was tearing her apart.

She traced those red lines, those precious words, with her fingertips, and then she put her head down on the page and wept.

Chapter Ten

The television cameras caught it all. The interview beforehand was concerned with the excellent draw he had made, meaning the bull with the rank reputation that he was about to ride, and his recovery from last year's injuries. The reporter followed him right up into the chute, jostling for position while Griff climbed onto the boards and lowered himself into place. The bull tried to break his legs before the gate was even opened, but Griff just kept smiling and lashed himself in place. Joan could not bear to think that he was actually tying his hand to that ferocious animal. Then he was pulling his hat down and winking at the camera, and the next thing she knew he was flying. The crowd roared as that bull whipped and snorted and generally tried to make mincemeat out of him, but he kept his free hand high, laid back and spurred that thick hide with both heels. The announcer was going crazy.

"What a ride! What a ride! The champion from Oklahoma is back!"

Joan hadn't known that so many eternities could be lived in eight seconds. She knew, and the announcer was busy telling her, that the most dangerous moments came after he hit the ground, which he did on his shoulder. But he rolled and came up on his feet, his hat in his hand. The bull went after him, but the bullfighter, the clown, intervened with a cleverly aimed, colored scarf shot from a toy gun. The bull reversed course and went after the clown. The man barely made it into the safety of a reinforced wood barrel before the bull tossed it onto its side and butted it. Meanwhile, Griff had reached the fence and climbed to safety. The hazers came in and drove the calming bull from the arena on their well-trained horses, while the clown went through his antics for the entertainment of the crowd and the announcer declared Griff's score. He was in first place, with four more riders to go.

Joan watched the next competitors with a critical eye. This one didn't lie back as far as Griff, that one flopped around like a rag doll. One was disqualified for some reason she didn't fully understand, and the last failed to make the buzzer and got stomped on in the bargain. Why anyone wanted to do such an insane thing as ride a bull in competition, she didn't know, but she felt the thrill of victory that must have been Griff's when it was announced that he had won! He waved to the crowd from atop the arena fence, then dropped to the ground to face yet another interview. Among the questions, he was asked if he would be going to a well-known bar in town for the traditional victory party.

Griff just laughed. "I'm heading for the airport. I'll celebrate when I get home." He took the time to talk about the school he was opening up and the rodeo stock he was going to breed on his ranch back in Oklahoma. Then he blew a kiss at the cameras, saying it was for "his girls," hoisted his gear and walked away. Joan went upstairs to tell Danna that

Griff had won and was on his way home. She hadn't allowed the child to watch the ride for fear that Griff would get hurt again right before her eyes, but Danna didn't know that. She jumped up at the news and danced around the bed, chanting, "Coming home! Coming home! Coming home! The champ! Wooo!"

He called when he reached the airport in Oklahoma City. Danna was asleep, but Joan had taken to sleeping in the master bedroom downstairs and so was near the phone. She snatched it up after the first ring. "Griff?"

"Hi, honey. I'm on the ground, safe and sound. We won!"

"I know. I was watching."

"Yeah? I didn't figure you for the sort to go with simulcast sports."

"I'm not."

"Ah. Well, we won't tell anyone. Wouldn't want a certain cowboy to get the wrong ideas, would we?"

"Don't be a dope."

"Not me, uh-uh. Hey, did I tell you that I miss you?"

"No."

"Well, I do, and I'd much rather be coming home to you than an empty house, but we won't quibble. Tell Danna I'll see her in the morning."

"In the morning? Not the afternoon?"

"In the morning," he said firmly. "Now turn in and get some sleep."

"That's what I was doing when you called," she retorted.

He laughed. "Right. On top of the phone, I guess."

She bristled. "If you think I was sitting here waiting—"

"Joan," he interrupted softly, "I love you, too." Then he made a kissing sound into the receiver and hung up.

She wanted to throw the thing across the room, but instead she found herself hugging the receiver to her chest. Then she dropped it into the cradle as if it was a hot potato. It was a funny thing, but after that call she fell soundly asleep, long before she could get through her litany of complaints about that high-handed, conceited Griff Shaw—who was coming home, safe and sound, a winner.

In the subsequent weeks, there was another ride and another win, then a loss, which seemed not to affect Griff at all. It was always the same; Griff went, he rode, he came home. Meanwhile, Frankie came home, too. She arrived from Florida with a walker and seemed to have aged ten years in as many weeks, but her spirit was intact. She was her same gruff, blunt, wonderful self, and she needed Joan as much then as Griff had needed her before. Joan threw herself into caring for her friend, and surprisingly it turned out to be a comfortable situation for everyone, including Griff, apparently, who seemed to be around most of time.

Yet, the school got built. Up went a small bunkhouse and a great blue sheet-metal structure with a maze of pipe fencing around a small arena. Horses were bought. Bulls were shipped in, including a mechanical one, and several cows, "good breeding stock," Griff called them. And, as hoped, the students began to sign on. Griff hired some hands to help out, hazers and wranglers, even a bullfighter. By spring they were in business, as he put it, and he was personally instructing his first class of fifteen hopeful young cowboys.

School was winding down for Joan and Danna just as Griff seemed busiest. Frankie exchanged the walker for a cane, and then the cane went into the corner and Frankie began creeping around on her own. One bright, crisp spring day that reeked of green, when afternoon made that pause that came just before the slide into evening, Joan made an early dinner. Everyone was starved for some reason or another. Frankie had expended a sudden burst of energy by pulling a few weeds out of the flower beds, but it had taken hours of outdoor play with neighborhood kids to take the edge off Danna's spring fever. Griff had spent the day with the contractor tearing a wall off his house and covering it up again with heavy sheets of plastic, while Joan had succumbed to the need to clean her classroom from top to bottom in a manner the custodial service would never dare duplicate. Appetites were sharpened to the point of slicing a few bellies, or so Griff claimed as he strolled into the kitchen. The beef tips were done, and the gravy was thickened. Water was boiling for the noodles, the bread was in the oven, and Joan was tossing a gargantuan salad with lemon and pepper dressing.

"I love a woman who can read my mind," he said, coming over to slide his arms around her waist from behind. "I could eat you, I'm so hungry, but then I always can."

"Cut it out, Griff," she chided unconvincingly, secretly thrilling as he squeezed her.

He nuzzled her ear through the cloud of her hair. "Um, you always smell so good."

She shoved an elbow at him without doing any damage, while her heart slammed like a sledgehammer against her own ribs. She closed her eyes briefly, awash with longing, but then she stiffened her spine and attempted to fend him off with a wiggle of her shoulders. "Frankie could walk in any minute," she scolded.

"And you think this would shock her?" He chuckled. "She knows what's what around here."

She had no doubt that he was right, considering the many knowing looks Frankie was always giving her, but she didn't have a better excuse. She couldn't very well tell him that he was driving her crazy and lowering her resistance just by standing close to her and sniffing her hair. "Just stop," she said shortly.

He sighed into her ear, giving her one more little squeeze, and said, "Okay, but don't kid yourself that she doesn't know what's going on."

"Nothing's going on."

He ignored her. "Where's Sunshine?"

"Washing up for dinner."

"Dinner, ooh, one of my favorite words."

She laughed, suddenly enjoying herself. "Fill the glasses, will you?"

He snapped a salute. "I live to serve." But the doorbell rang, and he did a smooth about-face. "I live to answer the door," he amended and hurried down the hall. She shook her head, enjoying this little bubble of happiness, which she swiftly attributed to spring fever.

She dumped the noodles in the water and set the timer, hearing voices and laughter from the foyer. She checked on the bread, turned off the oven and left the door ajar, then wandered down the hall. Who would be calling? Should she set another place for dinner?

She had just moved past the powder-room door when she heard Griff laugh and say, "Don't worry about it, guys. I still carry a little weight around here. Hey, what are you boys doing in Duncan anyway?"

"We came to see you!" a second male voice exclaimed. "You've been making some waves out there on the circuit again. We figured it was time to put the trio back together, get the old triple threat riding again."

"Not with this cowboy," Griff said. "Those days are over, boys, but hey, I haven't thanked you for bringing me home from Vegas! It was a dirty trick, getting me drunk like that, but I appreciate the delivery anyway."

There was the sound of slapping arms and shifting feet, then a voice that Joan now recognized as belonging to Casey Ashford asked, "Are you okay, Griff? Is there some left-over from that last bad wreck?"

"Naw, minor knee problem, nothing important. I've just rearranged my priorities, that's all."

"Priorities?"

"Mmm, hmm."

"You mean, there's something more important than rodeo?" This question came from a clearly confused Benny Butler, Joan was sure, and Griff confirmed it.

"Actually, Ben," Griff said, chuckling, "there are quite a few things more important than rodeo."

"Like what?" Benny wanted to know.

"Well, like family."

"Family?" It was a duet.

"You mean Grandma Frankie?" Casey asked.

"Partly."

A short silence followed, then Benny groaned. "Oh, Lord, you don't mean—"

"Congratulate me, boys!" said Griff in an amused, enthused voice. "I'm getting married."

The shock could not have been more palpable, for Joan *or* the boys. While she silently uttered a series of outraged expressions, several very blue words escaped someone else's lips.

"Watch that!" Griff snapped. "There's a kid here, not to mention the women."

"A kid!"

Joan didn't even try to identify who gasped that. She was too busy trying to get a handle on her feelings.

"I'll bet it's that sharp-tongued, hot-stuff redhead!" one of them exclaimed.

Joan pulled a face in outrage, but it wasn't sustainable as Griff came nimbly and instantly to her defense.

"Now, boys," Griff said calmly, too calmly, "you're old amigos and you're as welcome as rain in July, but you keep on like that and you're both gonna hit the street on your ears." Joan recognized that tone of resolve and couldn't help smiling.

Casey and Benny were not so sanguine. "The redhead," they confirmed in unison.

"Who'd a thought it?" said one.

"Well, I never!" said the other.

"And you won't, either," Griff announced flatly. "She'd chew you up and spit you out, both of you. Takes staying power to handle that much woman, but trust me, it's worth it. Now listen, dinner's on the table, and my backbone's been introduced to my belly button. You're welcome to stay, providing you behave yourselves and don't make me cut out your tongues."

"Won't Red object?" one of them asked.

Griff brushed aside his fears. "Naw, she's got claws, but at heart she's a pussycat."

"Oh, man, I'd stay on my best behavior for a week for a taste of Grandma Frankie's home cooking!" someone, probably Benny, promised.

Griff laughed. "Grandma's not cooking. She had a little wreck about the same time I did last year, and she's just now getting over it. But Jo lays a heck of a table, and she'll feed you if you don't embarrass her."

"Oh, no. Hey, we wouldn't," they both muttered almost incoherently, ". . . perfect gentlemen."

"That'll be the day!" Griff said good-naturedly. "Well, come on in. I'll get you something to drink, iced tea, maybe."

"Iced tea?" one of them whispered in horror. Then, without warning, they rounded the corner, and there she was, caught red-handed—red-faced anyway.

Griff's eyes widened, but then a knowing glint came into them and he recovered smoothly. "Honey," he said brightly, "you remember Casey and Ben, don't you?"

"Uh, er..." She cleared her throat. "That is, sure. Um, hi."

They both reached for hats they'd already hung on pegs in the foyer. "Nice to see you again... *Mrs. Shaw,*" Benny said meaningfully.

Griff grimaced and thumped him on the back of his head. "Not yet, fool!"

"Oh."

Casey made a better effort. "Best wishes to you, ma'am."

She dropped her gaze and willed away the heat in her cheeks, mumbling that best wishes were decidedly premature.

Griff distracted everyone by sliding his arm over her shoulders and turning her toward the kitchen. "You fellows can wash up right in there," he called out, pointing to the powder room as he ushered Joan down the hall. When they reached the kitchen door, he stopped and drew her around to face him. He sent a furtive look down the hall, then brought his face close to hers. "Don't humiliate me in front of my buds, honey, please," he pleaded in a whisper.

She should. She should have put an end to all this marriage talk right then and there, but somehow she just couldn't. She was having a devil of a time summoning up any anger these days where Griff Shaw was concerned; so instead of putting him firmly in his place once and for all, she simply frowned and nodded.

He smiled in relief, pulled her close and planted a kiss on her mouth. "I love you," he told her softly, and this time she didn't argue. What was the point after all?

Just then the timer went off, and she extracted herself from his grasp, announcing, "Dinner's ready."

He grinned, his eyes as soft as clouds, and said, "I'll get Frank and Danna."

She slipped away to quickly drain the noodles and set two more places at the table, while he knocked on Frankie's door and hollered up the stairs. Benny and Casey shuffled into the room awkwardly, and Joan promptly put them to work filling drinking glasses. Several busy moments later, Griff pulled her chair out for her and held it until she was seated, then those cowboys fell on the food like starving wolves. With the confidence of age and familiarity, Frankie reached out and wrapped Benny's knuckles with her butter knife.

"This is a God-fearing house," she said gruffly, her frown turning the wrinkles of her leathery face into a fearsome mask. "We don't eat till we pray. Now bow your scraggly heads." Though Frankie had previously done the praying aloud herself, this time she sent a meaningful look to Griff, who colored slightly and shifted uneasily in his chair.

Then he looked at Joan, and she saw, literally saw, the serenity that seemed to flow into him. Her heart was in her throat and, she feared, in her eyes when he reached for her hand. She bowed her head just to keep from looking at him and sat still while he said the brief words that blessed their meal. Afterward he leveled a look at Casey and Benny and said, "I'm getting good at this, boys. Hang around, you might learn something useful."

The boys seemed to be in shock. Benny's jaw was hanging. Frankie tore a piece off her dinner roll and shoved it into his mouth. Casey and Griff erupted in laughter. Danna gaped then threw back her head and cackled like a hen. Joan hid a smile, but couldn't contain her chuckles.

Tension banished, the cowboys once again attacked the food. Griff grinned, shrugged and waded in, but the plate he filled first was Danna's. Joan got to her feet and managed to snatch enough to feed herself and Frankie before the company gobbled up everything. What turned out to be a surprisingly pleasant half hour followed. And then Benny—naturally it was Benny—opened his mouth again and this time stuck his foot in it.

"So," he said with genuine interest, "when's the big day?"

Everyone at the table, with the possible exception of Danna, knew exactly what he was talking about. The quick glance that Frankie bounced between Griff and Joan announced clearly that she had no intention of coming to their aid. Griff picked up Joan's hand again, but without the glance—or the serenity.

"We, um, we're not sure. Things are pretty much up in the air right now, what with the school getting underway and... I'm building onto my house. Did I tell you that? I bought another house, well, a ranch. And, ah, the house was way too small, so just today, as a matter of fact, we ripped out the back wall and... well..."

He was floundering, this man who could ride bulls, overcome injuries and remake his life with ease, and Joan suddenly wanted fiercely to save him. Then the picture of those blocked-off dates in Griff's planner, outlined in red and with notes added in his own hand, popped into her head. It was meant to be a family holiday, but she couldn't help thinking that it would be a good time to get married. Nevertheless she was as shocked as anyone else when she heard herself say it. "July."

For just a moment, in the instant silence, she thought she'd imagined it, dreamed it, spun it out of some perverse need to torment herself. Then Griff's hand convulsed around hers and she recognized the astonishment he was trying to swallow. At that moment she realized fully what she'd done. She immediately started trying to undo it.

"I mean, J-July is . . . a good month."

"Good month for a wedding," Frankie said smoothly. "I've always thought so."

Joan thought Griff was going to break her hand. "Yeah," he said quickly, "everybody gets married in June. Why not July? Or May?"

May? "But May's too soon!" Joan gasped, and promptly blanched. What was she saying? What was she doing?

Griff was trying to plumb her gaze. "Right. Too soon. Ah, that's why we picked July." It came out almost as a question, but it was one Joan couldn't answer verbally.

"July's good," Casey muttered, looking slightly perplexed.

"Is it?" Griff asked softly, and he wasn't asking Casey. Joan could only shrug, hoping that was noncommittal enough to give him doubts. It wasn't. "July's wonderful!" Griff exclaimed, truly enthused now. "Heck, July's perfect! I always wanted to get married in July!"

"Married?" Danna echoed, her eyes growing large as the topic suddenly became clear to her. She whipped her head around to stare at Griff. "Yeah?" she asked hopefully.

Griff once more looked at Joan. This was her chance. All it needed was a negative expression, a carefully worded demur. She stared back like a dummy, practically catatonic. A tremulous smile stretched his mouth. "Married," he said.

Married. Twin bolts of fear and ecstasy shot through her. To her everlasting surprise, the ecstasy was far superior. Before she had time to contemplate that, Danna leapt up to nd on her chair and clapped her hands, chanting, "Oh, y! Oh, boy! We gettin' married. We gettin' married!" She pped and stared at Griff. "And 'dopted." Suddenly she gan to cry, her face crumpling up and big fat tears glid- down her cheeks.

"Danna!" Joan and Griff said it at the same time, but it s Griff who dropped Joan's hand and reached out for the ild.

She launched herself into his arms and buried her face in curve of his neck. "My daddy!" she wailed.

Griff turned a shocked, agonized face on Joan, and she ew they were both thinking the same thing. Dan Burton. iff pushed his plate away and sat Danna on the edge of table in front of him. "Honey? Danna? What's this out your daddy? I mean...I thought you understood that ant to be your daddy."

She lifted her little face and looked at him as if he had underhead" painted across his brow. "You *are* my ddy!" she exclaimed, wiping absently at the tears of joy at were vanishing as suddenly as they'd fallen. Then she oked at her mother. "I knew it all the time!" she vowed.

Joan was more perplexed than ever. "Danna," she said othingly, smoothing back her daughter's wild red hair, e've talked about this a lot. Remember? Your daddy's me is Daniel Burton, and he lives in—"

"No!" Danna interrupted. "Not that one! I mean my *real* ddy, the one that loves me! That's a real daddy, isn't it?"

"It is in my book," Frankie said complacently.

"Mine, too," Griff agreed firmly, his voice unusually ep and thick.

Danna wiped at her eyes again and looked at Joan. mething inside her crumbled, and with it went every fear d reservation she had. A father, a *real* father for her ughter, and a husband for her, a true husband, a loving, caring, determined husband, one with staying power. heart swelled as if it might burst. She gripped Griff's h and said, "Yes, baby, that's a real father."

Griff let his breath out in a rush, and then his arms coming around her and he was pulling her to him. leaned sideways on her chair and buried her face in the c of his shoulder as Danna had done and let herself enjoy the first time the comfort and protection and healing pc to be found there. He was laughing, or crying, or poss both. She wasn't sure which, but it didn't matter. All mattered was that they were bound together by a love surpassed anything she had ever known before. They family. In their hearts they were somehow already fami

"Oh, sweetheart," he whispered, "thank you. You w be sorry. As God is my witness, you won't be sorry!"

Joan put an arm around his neck and lifted her head know."

He kissed her right there at the dinner table, and might have gone on kissing if Danna had not brought tl back down to earth.

"How long is July?" she demanded.

"Not long," Frankie said.

Griff grinned against Joan's mouth and turned his h to insist, "Too long!"

"No, it isn't. It's just right," Joan said. "It'll be here fore you know it," she promised him, "and we won't long it. Let's say July 1. That ought to give us time to m Independence, don't you think?"

"I love you so much," he replied. It was the perfect swer, but Danna had her own ideas of perfection.

"Can I call you Daddy now?" she wanted to know.

"You better," Griff said with a laugh.

Danna beamed and got a combined hug from both G and Joan. They traded kisses all around. But then Danna back, narrowed her eyes and said, "Now when do I get my horse?"

It was the last thing either of them expected to hear—a perfectly normal, wonderfully selfish, completely childish thing to say—and after the initial surprise, it sent them both off in gales of laughter. Joan had no doubt they were remembering the same scene. Griff's suggestion, her indignation, Griff's ignominious capitulation, Danna's silent observance. Obviously neither had given her the credit she deserved. While they were fighting over emotional turf, she was banking on the eventual possession of that horse!

Through tears of absolute joy, Joan watched confusion cloud first Danna's face and then Benny's. But it was Benny who leaned over to his friend and whispered loud enough for the whole house to hear, "What's so funny about the kid wanting a horse? Don't every kid want a horse? I think they ought to buy her a horse."

Griff managed to get himself under control well enough to stutter, "Sh-she has a h-horse. I just h-haven't given it to her yet."

Joan's mental scenario vanished, replaced by raw, disconcerting truth. What had happened to her victory? She glared at Griff. "You bought her a horse? After I told you not to, you went ahead and bought her a horse?"

Griff sobered instantly. "Well, honey, it was a good buy and the right animal and . . . I didn't give it to her!"

"But you bought the horse!" Joan insisted. "How dare you buy the horse after I specifically told you not to?"

"I can buy a horse if I want to," he argued. "I wanted to have it handy when you finally came around."

Her mouth dropped open. "Pretty sure of yourself, weren't you? Of all the arrogant cowboys! What made you think—"

"Oh, no, you don't!" Griff suddenly sent his chair skittering back as he pushed up to his feet. He grabbed her hand and hauled her up after him. He clamped down on her shoulders and fixed her with a glare of his own. "I want a declaration right now and right here in front of witnesses."

She knew exactly what he meant, but for a moment she saw only red. "All right, I'll give you a declaration. You shouldn't have bought that horse!"

"Forget the danged horse!" he shouted. "I can buy any horse I want to, but that's not the issue. You're doing it again, Red, and this time I won't stand for it! Now tell me what I want to hear, blast you, or I'll...I'll...kiss you stupid!"

Well, that did it. Who could hang on to outrage in the face of that threat? But Joan gave it a valiant try. She huffed and tossed her gaze around and huffed some more, but finally she sighed. "I have a terrible temper," she muttered. "I never mean to—"

He shook her, just once, and brought his face close to hers. "I don't care about your blasted temper!" he said through his teeth. "You're a wildcat and I love it! We can fight every day and make up every night, as far as I'm concerned. Just do away with the damned smoke screens, Red. We don't need 'em. We need each other, and *I* need to hear you say it. Please."

The very real need in his eyes and voice convinced her. Her anger, without fear to maintain it, evaporated, and love once more flooded in to replace it. She lifted her hands to his face, looked deeply into his eyes and realized the truth, the whole truth. It was liberating to feel love again, but it was a revelation to feel the kind of love she had never felt before, not for Dan Burton, not for any man but this one. She smiled and said, "I love you, Griff Shaw, with every cell my body, every beat of my heart, and I'm sorry it took me so long to realize it."

He let go of her and put his head back in a long, loud sigh, pushed his hands over his face and shook a finger at her. "I'm gonna have me a belt buckle made," he said, "a great big, gaudy, gold-and-silver son of a gun that's gonna say, 'Red loves me!' By God, I've earned it, and it was the hardest won of the lot! And come July 1, woman, you better be at the church, or so help me I'm coming after you with a rope! Understand?"

She folded her arms, let the happy sweep of determination lift her ire and narrowed her eyes, ready to go toe-to-toe. "Oh, yes, I understand. You've won! Now I suppose you'll want to buy *me* a horse whether I want it or not!"

"I already have!" he flung back. "Now if you want to butcher it and make dog food out of it, be my guest, but by golly my daughter's gonna ride if she wants to ride, and that's the end of it!"

"Fine!" She threw her arms up. "After all, who am I to stand in the way?"

"You," he said, "are the most exasperating, hot-blooded, stubborn, enticing, lovable, wonderful *shrew* on the face of the earth. You're a dream come true, the mother of my children—and yes, that's plural—the most important thing that ever happened to me, and I love you with all my heart. So put that in your pipe and smoke it, Red! And come here."

He opened his arms, and she walked into them with a smile on her face, certainty and gratitude in her heart, and dreams bubbling inside her head, dreams she hadn't dared allow inside for so long, too long. She slid her arms around his waist and tilted her head back for his kiss, which, like everything else about him, exhibited amazing staying power. Once again she seemed to lose track of time and place and everything else but the man whose kisses she had both feared and coveted. It was Griff, reached by something or someone she had missed, who finally pulled back and cleared his throat. Irritated at the interruption, she turned her gaze around the room.

A grinning Danna stood next to Frankie, whose arm encircled her slender shoulders. Frankie's rather long, furrowed face crowned with silver had lost none of its dignity, but her pale blue eyes were swimming with unshed tears. She chucked Danna under the chin, then tapped the end of her nose, the picture of an indulgent but reasonable grandmother. Only Casey and Benny were openly gawking, those two bumbling miscreants who had nearly drowned an injured Griff in whiskey, dumped him on her floor and abandoned him, insulting her into the bargain. It seemed not only just to Joan that she target her irritation on them but also wise.

"Well?" she snapped.

Benny gulped. Casey reached for a hat that he wasn't wearing, then patted the top of his head as if to cover up that fact. "Uh, f-fine dinner, ma'am," he said lamely.

"Yeah, fine dinner!" Benny echoed.

"You won't mind cleaning up after yourselves then, will you?" she said pointedly. "I'd like a moment alone with my fiancé while you're at it."

She might have conked them both on the head with a hammer. Benny's eyes nearly popped out onto the floor, while Casey seemed to wilt, any pretense of bravado falling away like so many dead leaves on a winter day. Griff bit his lip, stifling amusement.

Frankie rose with obvious effort. "I think I'll spend a few minutes with my new granddaughter-to-be," she said with regal finality and shepherded Danna from the dining room.

Griff lifted an eyebrow at his friends, devoid of pity and brimming with amusement. "Claws," he reminded them, "soft heart but very sharp claws." Then he turned Joan and sent her toward the hallway with a little shove.

"Damn!" they heard Benny exclaim behind them.

"Hush your mouth," Casey hurriedly reprimanded, "or she'll have us mopping the floors next!"

"Her?" Benny complained. "What about Griff? What d'you suppose has happened to him? It ain't healthy, giving up bad habits cold turkey like that."

"Cold turkey?" Griff mused, hustling Joan into Frankie's room and taking her into his arms once more. "More like a red-hot cat!" And he proceeded to make her burn, claws sheathed, heart open, until he had her purring as only a man with his uniquely winning way could do.

* * * * *

Get Ready to be Swept Away by
Silhouette's Spring Collection

Abduction & Seduction

These passion-filled stories explore both the dangerous desires of men and the seductive powers of women. Written by three of our most celebrated authors, they are sure to capture your hearts.

Diana Palmer
Brings us a spin-off of her Long, Tall Texans series

Joan Johnston
Crafts a beguiling Western romance

Rebecca Brandewyne
New York Times bestselling author
makes a smashing contemporary debut

Available in March at your favorite retail outlet.

Silhouette®

ABSED

MILLION DOLLAR SWEEPSTAKES (III)

No purchase necessary. To enter, follow the directions published. Method of entry may vary. For eligibility, entries must be received no later than March 31, 1996. No liability is assumed for printing errors, lost, late or misdirected entries. Odds of winning are determined by the number of eligible entries distributed and received. Prizewinners will be determined no later than June 30, 1996.

Sweepstakes open to residents of the U.S. (except Puerto Rico), Canada, Europe and Taiwan who are 18 years of age or older. All applicable laws and regulations apply. Sweepstakes offer void wherever prohibited by law. Values of all prizes are in U.S. currency. This sweepstakes is presented by Torstar Corp., its subsidiaries and affiliates, in conjunction with book, merchandise and/or product offerings. For a copy of the Official Rules send a self-addressed, stamped envelope (WA residents need not affix return postage) to: MILLION DOLLAR SWEEPSTAKES (III) Rules, P.O. Box 4573, Blair, NE 68009, USA.

EXTRA BONUS PRIZE DRAWING

No purchase necessary. The Extra Bonus Prize will be awarded in a random drawing to be conducted no later than 5/30/96 from among all entries received. To qualify, entries must be received by 3/31/96 and comply with published directions. Drawing open to residents of the U.S. (except Puerto Rico), Canada, Europe and Taiwan who are 18 years of age or older. All applicable laws and regulations apply; offer void wherever prohibited by law. Odds of winning are dependent upon number of eligibile entries received. Prize is valued in U.S. currency. The offer is presented by Torstar Corp., its subsidiaries and affiliates in conjunction with book, merchandise and/or product offering. For a copy of the Official Rules governing this sweepstakes, send a self-addressed, stamped envelope (WA residents need not affix return postage) to: Extra Bonus Prize Drawing Rules, P.O. Box 4590, Blair, NE 68009, USA.

SWP-S295

This February from

Silhouette ROMANCE™

Sister Switch

by

Carolyn Zane

When twin sisters switch identities, mischief, mayhem—and romance—are sure to follow!

UNWILLING WIFE

(FEB. '95 #1063)

Erica Brant agreed to take her sister's place as nanny for two rambunctious children. But she never considered that their handsome single father would want to make *her* his new bride!

WEEKEND WIFE

(MAY '95 #1082)

When a sexy stranger begged Emily Brant to pose as his wife for the weekend, it was an offer she couldn't resist. But what happens when she discovers he wants more than just a pretend marriage?

Don't miss the fun as the Brant sisters discover that trading places can lead to more than they'd ever imagined. SISTER SWITCH—only from Silhouette Romance!

SSD1

WHERE THE HEART IS

Don't miss the final book in
this heartwarming series from

ELIZABETH AUGUST

A HUSBAND FOR SARAH

Sam Raven had teased and challenged Sarah Orman as a girl, now he dared her to accept his wild proposal. Would Sarah's lifelong rival become her lifetime love?

WHERE THE HEART IS: With her wit and down-to-earth charm, Sarah Orman always had a way of bringing couples together. Now she finds a romance of her own!

Available in March, only from

Silhouette
ROMANCE™

WTH-1

SILHOUETTE... Where Passion Lives

Don't miss these Silhouette favorites by some of our most distinguished authors! And now you can receive a discount by ordering two or more titles!

SD#05786	QUICKSAND by Jennifer Greene	$2.89	☐
SD#05795	DEREK by Leslie Guccione	$2.99	☐
SD#05818	NOT JUST ANOTHER PERFECT WIFE by Robin Elliott	$2.99	☐
IM#07505	HELL ON WHEELS by Naomi Horton	$3.50	☐
IM#07514	FIRE ON THE MOUNTAIN by Marion Smith Collins	$3.50	☐
IM#07559	KEEPER by Patricia Gardner Evans	$3.50	☐
SSE#09879	LOVING AND GIVING by Gina Ferris	$3.50	☐
SSE#09892	BABY IN THE MIDDLE by Marie Ferrarella	$3.50 U.S. ☐ $3.99 CAN.	☐
SSE#09902	SEDUCED BY INNOCENCE by Lucy Gordon	$3.50 U.S. ☐ $3.99 CAN.	☐
SR#08952	INSTANT FATHER by Lucy Gordon	$2.75	☐
SR#08984	AUNT CONNIE'S WEDDING by Marie Ferrarella	$2.75	☐
SR#08990	JILTED by Joleen Daniels	$2.75	☐

(limited quantities available on certain titles)

	AMOUNT	$______
DEDUCT:	10% DISCOUNT FOR 2+ BOOKS	$______
	POSTAGE & HANDLING ($1.00 for one book, 50¢ for each additional)	$______
	APPLICABLE TAXES*	$______
	TOTAL PAYABLE (check or money order—please do not send cash)	$______

To order, complete this form and send it, along with a check or money order for the total above, payable to Silhouette Books, to: **In the U.S.:** 3010 Walden Avenue, P.O. Box 9077, Buffalo, NY 14269-9077; **In Canada:** P.O. Box 636, Fort Erie, Ontario, L2A 5X3.

Name:______________________________

Address:____________________ City:____________

State/Prov.:________________ Zip/Postal Code:____________

*New York residents remit applicable sales taxes.
Canadian residents remit applicable GST and provincial taxes.

SBACK-DF

Silhouette®